A PRAYER FOR TOBIAS

HOW A FRIGHTENED, HOMELESS DOG IS SAVED BY AN ANGEL
AND HOW HE BECOMES AN ANGEL HIMSELF.

TOBIAS BOOK I

BOBBI BOLAND WHITE

WingSpan Press

Published in the United States and the United Kingdom by WingSpan Press, Livermore, CA

The WingSpan name, logo and colophon are the trademarks of WingSpan Publishing.

ISBN 978-1-59594-609-6 (pbk.)

First edition 2017

Printed in the United States of America

www.wingspanpress.com

Library of Congress Control Number 2017945492

1 2 3 4 5 6 7 8 9 10

FOR ALL OF THE ANGELS WHO COME WHEN WE CALL

CHAPTER 1

He came out of the wasteland like a phantom, barely able to see, a shadow, his skin hanging in folds, his coat thin and matted, the wound in his chest a deep circle of scarlet brown. But it was his eyes that weakened her, drove her to her knees – eyes that were empty, opaque with pain, eyes that were white like the sky was white.

The rumor was that he was dead – had died two years ago outside the iron gates of the abandoned property where he once lived. For weeks no one had noticed him; the steady rains had beaten down the saffron leaves of autumn under which he lay, his silken coat no longer ruffled by the early winter winds that blew in from the sea, his ears folded and still, closed like his eyes to the coldness of the world.

An officer had finally picked up the body. He cradled it gently, put it in his van and took it to the place where bodies found abandoned were checked for disease and then assigned to ashes or weighed down and sent to rest beneath the sea.

He told the young girl he was sorry; animals were difficult to see in the heavy fog that often cloaked the coastal road. Perhaps, he said, someone had seen him when the fog had lifted, stopped and dragged his body over to the gate. She would find another dog, he said, looking at the photo she had handed him, his heart aching at the loss in her eyes, turning away.

She had stood in shock at the end of the long driveway, the iron gates ajar, her stomach dropped, her legs weak. She had walked up to the empty house, seen the dirt encrusted on the rim of the overturned dish that once was his, the layer of white lime that formed a chalky coating on what used to be his water bowl.

"Maybe they took him with them when they moved," her friend had said. "Maybe the dog on the road was another dog."

But Mira knew they hadn't taken him. She knew that he had been weeks and weeks alone in that yard. He wasn't as pretty as their purebred dogs and he was far too shy to properly protect their property. And yet they told her that he would be safe with them, that he would learn to guard their home and she could always call to check on him.

But Mira knew that something wasn't right; she begged and begged her father to go back for him, but Jacob always pleaded for more time – just one more month, he had told her, just six more months. So she had researched carefully how she could go alone, catch the 707 from the university where her father worked and where she and her brother lived with him in the "no pets allowed" apartment.

The trip from Union Station up the California coast was only $40 dollars and by noontime she was walking … walking … walking up the old familiar roads "How did you do it?" her friend had asked, "How could you board the train alone like that? Didn't they question your age, check your I.D?"

"They didn't even notice me," Mira said, I just slipped in with some older kids. But, anyway, I changed my birthdate, just to be safe. "See?" she had said, digging out the altered card.

"Wow," her friend had said, taking the card and peering down at it, "you moved it up to 16? Just like that? Weren't you scared of getting caught?"

But Mira wasn't listening anymore, just walking along, checking the scattered yards and houses for the dog she knew would not be there. "I told him," she said quietly, "to wait for me. I told him I'd come back for him."

He stopped believing, she was thinking, taking back her I.D. card, smiling at her friend, he stopped believing I would ever come. I need to just get over it, she told herself. I need to think of other things. Like the officer had said, like her father would say, like everyone would tell her, she should look to the future; she'd find another dog someday."

"Yeah, you're right. I guess that's what I'll have to do," she would say to her father, to everyone.

Again and again she'd pretend to agree, pretend she had accepted their advice, that she was being sensible and "moving on." But it wasn't true.

Because, throughout the months, the years that followed, whatever else that Mira did, she knew beyond a doubt that her Tobias wasn't dead. She knew it in the way the heart knows. No mater how hopeless it looked, he wasn't dead. If his life were to be meaningless, cut short on an empty storm drenched road, he would have died when he had been abandoned the first time, tossed from the window of a moving car, just a pup, broken and bruised, huddled in the weeds until she had found him and taken him home.

She had lived with him for almost a year before the family had to move, before she was told she had to give him up. And in that year she had spoken to his soul and he had spoken to hers. So Mira knew for certain, beginning that day as she bid her friend good-by, that wherever Tobias was, he was alive.

That's all that really matters, God, she prayed as she boarded the train back to the city – that he's alive, that you're protecting him. "Even if we never see him again," she told her younger brother, Ben, later that night, when she was finally home and on her way to bed, "it's okay because, at least so far, I'm sure – sure to the bone that he's alive."

And she was right.

CHAPTER 2

But it had been a close call for Tobias. He knew the people who had left him didn't want him anymore; he knew that he had disappointed them – acting silly all the time, wandering off for days, forgetting that he had a job to do.

So once he realized that this was it, that they were never coming back, Tobias stood alone by the shuttered house and looked around. His future, like the vacant property surrounding him, loomed grey and frightening. He had the strangest feeling that his life was almost over now, that soon his body would be underground, walled in with dirt and stone.

Well, Tobias shook his head, it wasn't over yet. He would surprise them all; he would protect this yard with all his might, and if no one ever came for him he would still protect it, maybe forever.

And so Tobias got to work. He dug a hiding place, a shallow bed behind the gates where he could not be seen.

And there he waited, day after day, just looking out, waiting to surprise a would-be trespasser. Now, he felt, he was the guard dog that he was supposed to be.

Tobias seldom moved from his bed of leaves that fall, even when the rains began. Sometimes it rained all day, a steady, drenching rain that soaked his coat and soaked his makeshift hiding place.

And yet he stayed right where he was, not even bothering most days to look for food – a big mistake because the early winter nights were getting cold, filled with howling wind and fog, and even when there was no fog the sky lay thick and black and silent on the road so that he dared not venture out upon it.

Until one night he heard a thump; a car pulled up and stopped just down the road. Tobias shook himself awake; his heart was pounding as he tried to stand. For a few minutes he listened. Then slowly he left his bed and walked outside the gate. He couldn't see; fog covered everything. Tobias' leg was trembling but he took another step, then two.

Suppose there was another creature, just like him, who had been hurt, someone hiding close-by from the rain, some-one who was also frightened and alone. But looking through the endless fog, there wasn't anyone that he could see; there was no movement on the road at all, just one dark shape that could be anything: some trash, some branches blown there from the wind.

Tobias sighed. He should admit the truth. It wasn't trash. But even if he knew before it happened, there was no way he could have stopped it. He was too weak; he took too long get up from his bed.

Tobias hung his head; his shoulders sank as he turned around to re-enter the yard. And so, because Tobias didn't know what else to do, he offered up his life – whatever might be left of it, to anyone at all who might know how to do a better job with it – a better job than he had done so far. And then he sighed again, lay down and closed his eyes. And then the angel came.

Until that night, Tobias had never personally met an angel. He knew that Mira spoke to one in whispers, especially when she was worried about something. Angel of God, my Guardian dear, she would pray, closing her eyes in order to see the angel more clearly because although these amazing beings had other ways to make their presence known, an actual glimpse of one was rare.

Angels, it seemed to Tobias, were a big help in times of trouble. However, as a result of his observations, Tobias had always assumed that angels were sent exclusively to humans. He never imagined that an angel would be interested in *him*, would want to help *him*.

But there she was, surprising him with her energy, her gentleness, urging him up and out of his bed, trotting beside him as he looked around and shook the leaves from his coat.

It was a glorious dawn, no fog, no rain, and just the two of them trotting along the empty road. So that all at once, for no reason he could understand, Tobias felt … well, better, much better. He even felt taller! Somehow the angel had made him feel new again – was it possible? Because that's how he felt, brand new and filling up with happiness, silly with it, bursting with it!

Tobias slowed and let her move ahead. For a moment he looked at her – wow, an angel! Suddenly, without warning, Tobias' happiness took hold of him and he was running with the angel not behind her, crashing into her with friendly bumps and nudges, ecstatic to have company again, down the long hill to the coast, jumping in and out of the foaming tide, always turning to make sure she was there.

She helped him search for food, for tidbits washed up by the sea, and best of all she played with him, leaping over stones and driftwood, zigzagging over quilts of jellyfish that were pale blue, translucent on the cool sand.

She would slow down and move beside him to approach with caution those huge mounds of seeming stone – napping seals with trunks like elephants that could move suddenly and come alive, lift up their massive heads or never move at all but simply open one enormous eye to warn them not to come that way.

But winter wasn't over as they traveled down the California Coast. Wind bit at them and roared around them in the night, pushing them up through the jagged rocks, forcing them inland to the rivers and the greening hills that rolled for miles toward the middle of the state.

She was leading him east. Sometimes she would be so far ahead that he would bark to her, complain that he could not keep up. Then, the moment that he saw her, he would leap forward again, bounding happily along, his long tail waving behind him.

He was no hunter yet, preferring winter fruits and berries, small birds blown out of trees. But he was fine. What mattered was he had a friend. Finally. A real friend like Mira had been, a friend that he could count on when he needed her.

But then one day, everything changed. The angel sat down beside Tobias and gave him the message she had come to give. It was a serious message and Tobias listened intently. An innocent man would need his help. He must find this man. He must not falter if he found himself alone. Ready or not, he must go on.

Tobias understood the angel but he was afraid. When would she leave him? How would he know what to do without her? He was paying strict attention to her now, watching her every move, and soon he noticed that he had indeed learned many things from her. He would stand tall and scan the fields and roads for hidden dangers that could threaten them, and if there were no danger Tobias would pretend that there was one – just to show how brave he had become.

Then one morning when Tobias awoke he was no longer afraid. And the pretending stopped. And the angel was gone.

He was in grazing country then, trotting up and down the slopes where cattle who had left the group and ventured out alone would turn to look at him in shock, recovering soon to realize that he was certainly not a predator with his long tangled tawny coat and ears that flopped over rather than standing up like those of a coyote or a wolf.

Often, Tobias would join the cattle, moving freely among them, nuzzling up against their thick legs. Their breath was warm; Tobias felt safe with them.

But winter was ending and there were new concerns among these friends of his, tiny shivering bundles suddenly appearing everywhere, barely visible in the straw-like grass. And Tobias knew by instinct it was time to go. Their lives were wrapped around this place, each other, and this land. But his was not. He must move on.

* * *

Throughout the summer Tobias continued his journey east, avoiding towns and traffic, veering south, crossing miles of farmland, tugging at the tops of baby beets, pulling carrots from the ground and chewing on them with delight.

Dawn would find him right at home on someone's cultivated land, chomping on snap peas, just sailing happily along, his tail waving in the breeze. There were no fences, and there were no predators. How could he know that it would not last?

So he went on, still veering south, aware of highways, roads and traffic that he must avoid, traveling down the long sweet smelling orchards that seemed to fill the middle of the state.

Of course it wasn't always easy to find food. Eggplant, summer squash and melons were plentiful but often they refused to open up for him; he would roll them, shake them and pounce on them. Finally, he'd stop to catch his breath, select the one that had most seriously defied him and give it a royal pee.

Change came slowly. The sky paled; there was less and less to eat; acres of land lay brown and empty. Often, his stomach growled painfully and he began to consider moving closer to the barns and homes he passed. But Tobias had learned to be shy of humans. Only once did a warning shot catch him by surprise, whizzing over his head on a quiet night. But once was enough.

Other lessons were more painful – comical perhaps to the farmer who watched, but not so funny to Tobias. One morning, as he was trotting down a narrow road, his hunger making sleep impossible, he noticed a span of acreage filled with low plants that seemed to offer small white balls of fruit, just emerging from their pods and ripe for eating.

Tobias plunged into the field and hungrily chomped down on one of these plants without his usual investigative sniff. Cotton! His mouth was filled with it, sticking to his teeth, his gums, the roof of his mouth, even his tongue. He pawed at it. He ran from it. He filled his mouth with muddy water, chewed leaves and sticks and spit them out, glad for once the angel wasn't there to see him slink away.

Or was she? Tobias looked around furtively. Maybe she was hiding from him, watching from a distance. What kind of friend was that?

He was losing weight rapidly. Almonds filled the orchards that he traveled through, pistachios and cherries were plentiful. But it didn't matter; they hurt his stomach if he ate more than a few, and grapes although plentiful were even worse, a poison that he could not tolerate.

Tobias' stomach yearned for more substantial food. His mouth watered as the smell of barbecued steak or ribs drifted across the autumn nights. More than once he waited as the lights blinked out in a humble home.

He had become a shadow, snooping through their trash and garbage silently, his trophy of half-eaten bread a sorry prize for taking such a foolish risk.

And after all, it didn't help – not much. In fact, it didn't really help at all.

Tobias didn't know how to pray – not as we do. But he did know how to hope. He was busy doing just that – hoping, when he noticed the children. It was early September now and groups of boys and girls could be seen waiting with their backpacks at bus stops all along the country roads.

Tobias would sit down a short distance from them and give his best, most hopeful look, wagging his tail at whoever looked his way. Best of all, these wags and hopeful looks were genuine. Tobias delighted in children; just seeing them, watching them play, made him happy.

After all, a child like one of these had given him the only love that he had ever known. So he would smile willingly at them, walk over when they called and gladly sniff each out-stretched hand. And they reciprocated, not only with laughs and pets, but also with apples, peanut butter sandwiches, and cookies.

But then, one day after the bus had left, Tobias felt a twinge of guilt. He had some thinking to do and he knew it. He moved beneath a spreading tree by the side of the road and lay down on the carpet of leaves beneath it.

All summer he had been avoiding the cities to his east. Industry had frightened him: trains and smoke, tall buildings and long yards of trucks, chain link fences with circles of razor wire on top. But now those scents and images were gone. The land had opened up; the air was clean. It wasn't right to linger here.

Tobias emerged from under his tree and walked to a clearing. It was true the city images were gone, but in their place he noticed hills to his east, hills that seemed to climb and crawl forbiddingly, folding into rifts and gullies, shadowed and ominous. Perhaps if he continued south and just ignored them for a while, they too would disappear, like the cities.

Tobias began to walk. But then he stopped. The land that stretched before him to the south was empty now, stripped of its crops, stark and frightening. The children were gone.

And suddenly without warning a sense of desolation entered the soul of Tobias. Where was the angel when he needed her? What would she do if she were here? Where would she lead him?

But of course he knew.

Tobias trudged eastward. The hills before him had become mountains. The wind pushed at him and hurt his eyes so that he closed them often as he walked slowly up the narrow roads and trails.

He had not gone far, less than a mile, when he heard the gunshots. They were well above him, yet something was urging Tobias to pause, to go no further.

He waited. He listened. He began to climb more slowly. He followed a trail that led him into some protective trees and then, rounding a steep bend in the trail, he looked down.

A few cattle were huddled together in a valley below him. He was so glad to see them. It made no sense, but all he wanted was to be close to them. Cautiously he started down the steep grade. There would be wind and mud with which to deal on the valley floor but Tobias sensed correctly that where the wind howled, gunshots could not be heard, and that was good.

As before, the cattle accepted Tobias. They knew, these wise ones, that even more than food Tobias needed company, and so they granted it. The wind was easier to bear with friends around, and when the wind was cold Tobias would lie down among them, and he would close his eyes as they did, and submit to it.

For several days Tobias stayed in the valley. He was still

hungry, massively hungry, but at least he was safe. Then, on the third day, Tobias roused himself from sleep.

It was quiet – no wind. He stretched. He must be brave. What if the angel were watching? She believed in him, didn't she? He must be strong for her. Until his mission was complete, he must go on.

And so, alone once more, as winter darkened the skies above him, heavy with slate blue clouds that hung low over his head, Tobias moved up from the valley and deeper into the hills of Tehachapi.

CHAPTER 3

December. Stallion Springs. Tobias breathed deeply. There were no gunshots now, only homes and ranches scattered about, and whenever he warily approached one and was seen, he was amazed to find food left out for him, bones and buckets of water.

Wildlife seemed to be everywhere, tempting him to give chase – ducks and wild geese honking and flapping over natural ponds and lakes. And there were apples – red and green and yellow, ripe and delicious hiding under russet leaves, rolling under fences, stopping at his feet.

Tobias was relieved. The sky above him was the deepest blue. His coat had thickened and even on the coldest days he roamed the fields between barns and ranches without fear. He crossed bridges, drank from icy creeks and he slept long and peaceful nights in culverts deep between the sloping hills as mountain snows blew over him.

It was too good to last, wasn't it? You bet it was.

Spring awakened Tobias with a start. It had been one year since the angel had come for him. What was he doing? But as Tobias prepared to resume his journey, he was in for a shock.

As he emerged, tall and rested from the flowering hills of Tehachapi, he saw to his east an astounding sight: great empty stretches of dry land, rolling mounds of earth without a single tree that marched to the horizon where tall iron sentinels stood like frozen scarecrows in rows against the sky, their empty heads holding long blades that spun round and round in the white wind.

Tobias turned back. He closed his mind to it. He moved down to a canyon at the foot of the hills and crossed the road that ran through it. The land was greener on this other side and Tobias began to follow the paths of other animals that had gone north, just trotting along the gentle slopes, eating grass, pretending everything was fine.

For two more weeks Tobias denied the emptiness that lay to his east. He continued north, experienced forests and winding trails. He begged successfully for food at a Buddhist temple deep in the hills and lay listening to the music of its bells. He liked it there. He liked it very much and so, being the curious fellow that he was, Tobias walked right into the temple itself one day. He just sat down and rested there, and for a long time he thought about things.

Tobias stayed at the temple for almost a week. He played along the wooded paths, ate leaves and berries, chased rabbits and gophers. But more and more his curiosity was itching him. Whatever it was out there, he had to know.

The air was warmer as he headed east. Occasionally he could see between the hills – a sliver of sky. The light was brilliant there; it hurt his eyes. And then one day he saw it all: miles and miles of blinding light. And heat. Heat that rose before him like a wall. The Mojave.

For one more day Tobias strode the hilltops as the desert stretched and sizzled below him. He rolled against some rocks, wiggling and then standing again and shaking, as his winter fur flew off in tufts, lifting his head in pride at this accomplishment, feeling strong and capable.

The angel had been his friend when he had no other. He would continue as she had instructed.

Tobias began his journey across the Mojave in June, a trek just short of 300 hundred miles, east … north … then east again. He detoured often, sometimes looking for food or sometimes simply sniffing after unfamiliar scents.

His path, once he turned north, would be blocked by hills of jagged rock and steep canyons of forbidding darkness, yet in spite of this, the endless barren miles he faced as he trod east, the burning unforgiving emptiness that stretched before him, was worse. And soon Tobias' thirst was huge and his bones ached and his head was hot.

But he went on.

In July, he began to travel only at night, burrowing underground during the day. He would look for rocks and dig between them, or down beneath them, looking for shade. Often he disturbed the pocket of a sleeping snake and would be forced to stop his digging and back up respectfully.

But the snakes were good teachers and Tobias learned to find his own place of relief by searching carefully as they had done, by going deep and angling into coolness only after long and patient struggles with the desert floor.

He learned how difficult it was to catch the desert mice and lizards that came out at dawn. He tried and tried, anxious, racked with hunger, pouncing, digging, collapsing and covering his eyes in frustration and shame.

Death Valley. Mountains ahead. Waterless ravines. Shadowed chasms.

Learning to conserve his strength, learning to stay back and to observe the desert dwellers that he couldn't catch and, rather than pounce upon them, learning to slink down like a shadow on the desert floor and follow them.

This way he discovered what was safe to eat. He learned the healing powers of the magical mesquite. Not only the leaves and pods but also the bark of the mesquite, like that of the desert willow, could be chewed upon to bring relief from cuts and scrapes and aching bones.

But of all that Tobias learned that summer, nothing amazed him more than the secret of coyote wells. It happened one morning in full light. Tobias was resting under some desert scrub when he saw a rare sight, the angled form of long legged coyote trotting past him in a direct line toward a scraggly bush a short distance away.

As Tobias watched, peering out from his protected cover, the coyote began to purposefully dig beneath the bush; he dug and dug, head and shoulders disappearing, rump high, tail slowly swinging back and forth.

Consumed with curiosity, when the coyote emerged and went his way Tobias slinked over to the scraggly bush and stuck his nose down in the hole. It was cool! It smelled of water! Tobias pawed more deeply and then water appeared – an inch of water … and then … more water! In this way Tobias discovered the wonder of coyote wells. And he drank his fill and was refreshed.

But still, he needed food. He was often dizzy and his vision sometimes blurred so that even when a mouse or gopher ran right past him, many times he was too weak to catch it. Until at last, struggling through the dreary miles of empty land, it dawned upon him that the only key to catching anything that moved, was simply not to move himself – to just be still.

And so, alone on Earth's most desolate terrain, Tobias sat sometimes for hours, as still as stone beneath the desert sky, blending in his tawny coat with miles of barren land, tall straw-like reeds and rocks that lay where ancient riverbeds once lay but now had dried, cracking into squares that led like sidewalks into nowhere.

Tobias would wait. He was doing his best to trust the universe – to trust that it would see his need, and balance and consider it. Until at last the air would cool; the sun would spread her robes of gold and bronze across his eyes, his coat, his paws, and so distract him as his meal moved slowly out before him, and stopped there, to present itself.

This was not the only way Death Valley embraced Tobias and gave up her secrets, but it was the best one.

Often, there were no coyote wells, no secret pools to quench the burning in his throat. At first, Tobias drew a small supply of moisture from the swollen cactus leaves, the lizards and the roots he ate. But it was never enough and sometimes, after a bite or two, his throat hurt even more..

And yet Tobias knew he must go on. He knew that his was not the only shadow moving through the desert night. His strength had ebbed and yet he knew instinctively the value of his tortured flesh to other solitary hunters that stalked unseen, as he did, far and wide beneath the fullness of a moon that hid nothing, and that placed no life with more importance than the next.

August. Early fall. Tobias lifted his head to the fine mist of a desert rain. And the rain blessed him and cooled him. So that his gratitude was huge and loud as he stopped, sat down, and sang his heartfelt thanks to a universe that could not help but hear it.

But it was still the Mojave and Tobias was still a little more than walking death. Often he had lost his way, blinded by a blazing, unrelenting sun that scarred his vision even as he turned away from it and lowered his gaze as other creatures did, letting his eyelids close to slits.

Autumn was a relief, yes. But the great expanse of desert floor still blurred before Tobias' eyes. And he tripped often as he climbed through the rocks and roots of Death Valley's eastern rim.

A brave and solitary figure, he made his way across the final canyon and started up a long and empty trail into the brown hills of Western Nevada.

CHAPTER 4

Tobias had survived Death Valley but the journey had taken a terrible toll. The pads on his feet were torn and crusted black with blood so that he limped slowly among the miles of deserted mines, their boarded entrances crumbling, no longer needed to keep thieves away, no longer good for anything – like him.

When evening came, Tobias wrapped himself around and closed his eyes, pressed back in the dark cave of an abandoned mine – hungry, exhausted, alone.

That winter Tobias experienced a hunger that his heart had never known, a terrible emptiness. Every dawn, he would lie at the mouth of his lonely cave, and he would study the coyotes loping in silence through the early light below. They were so much like him – the way they moved, the silent way they paused and turned to look at him. They also were lonely. They also suffered.

Even when he never saw them, he could hear them; he could hear their prayers, their calling out across the night, across the low clouds, across the lifespan of a planet that had known them for a million years. Their prayers seemed familiar to Tobias – like an ancient song buried deep in his memory and he would often fall asleep to this song.

He longed to meet a coyote, to touch one. However they mostly traveled in pairs, slowing briefly to acknowledge him, then moving on. It was not until the winter's coldest days that he noticed a change.

As he walked slowly through the rocky land, down into dry canyons looking for a trickle of water, a morsel of food, the few coyotes that he passed seemed much more docile than before, more accepting of him, more respectful of his chosen path.

He was taller than most of them, yet much thinner. Perhaps they could tell that he was getting old, a sad cousin on the same brief path as theirs through life, his coat hanging loosely on bones that were swollen, brittle, near starvation but proudly enduring his hunger, at home on the brown land, privileged to have had his few Springs, learned his few lessons, beaten down by loneliness, ravaged by the elements, but still not ready to succumb.

And then one morning, a female came to him. She looked silently at Tobias, appearing at the edge of his cave, her golden eyes clear and questioning. He had no idea what to do, and so he stood and took one step toward her and stopped. She cautiously began to circle him, slowly moving ever closer while he stayed rigid and still, trembling slightly but not understanding why he trembled.

And then, carefully, she touched him, laid her head lightly on his back, breathing gently into his fur. Tobias could feel her heartbeat; that's how close to him she stood. He turned his head to her ever so slightly and then she did the most amazing thing: she looked up at him and gave him her breath. It was clean and fresh – a sweetness that dove within him to a place he could not name, had never experienced.

She backed up quickly then and just before she disappeared she paused, the sky a cobalt blue behind her. And it seemed to Tobias that she smiled at him, that her eyes smiled. Maybe she did. Or maybe not. It was a look, however, that she wrote on his heart, and he would treasure it throughout his life, and even beyond it.

He dreamed of her that night, dreamed that she came to him again and lay against him. When he awoke he still sensed her, and he pawed at the dirt where she had lain in his dream, and he could feel her all about him.

But she was gone, and a great emptiness opened within Tobias, and he felt that he could not go on. He had obeyed the angel. He had done his best. But for Tobias the end seemed near. Weariness had halted his journey, pressed in upon him dulling his eyes, weighing his shoulders low to the ground. And every muscle ached. And his heart within him ached.

Tobias experienced only one human contact that winter in the brown hills, moving slowly from the shelter of one abandoned mine to the next, but it was a welcome one and it reminded him of that which Mira had taught him long ago – that strangers sometimes could be kind.

Mira herself had been so kind to him, stroking his fur and giving him milk and small bits of food from her hand. She had played with him, taken him on long walks, and promised she would never leave him.

But she must have forgotten that promise because one day she took him to a long yard that reached all the way to the sea where he was expected to guard the property of humans whom he did not know, humans who did not love him. She told him that he must be good and wait for her. "Stay. Toby," she had told him. "Stay."

But the yard had been a lonely place for Tobias and once he discovered several hidden spots along the fence where he could dig, he tunneled out to look for her. Month after month he ranged across the land, traveling up and down the country roads searching … searching … always for her. Where was she? Where had she gone?

Crushed with failure, each time he would return to the yard and crawl back under the fence. Perhaps if he stayed there long enough, she would come back for him. But she never did.

And then, after almost a year of waiting for Mira, even these who did not love him abandoned him. He saw them go, watched the moving trucks go down the driveway in a line. At first he thought they would return. He paced. He checked his food and water bowls.

For many days and many nights he tried to guard the empty property for them, but he was weak from hunger and once the rains began he wasn't able even to do that. So he had lay down by the gate one final time and closed his eyes, until the angel came.

But now, as Tobias looked down from his cave and saw the human walking alone, shouldering a backpack, investigating all the nooks and hidden tunnels to the mines below, he felt the heart within him surge with hope. He knew it could be dangerous to reveal himself. He knew this stranger could decide to capture or to kill him.

But the need in the heart of Tobias outweighed his fears and outweighed his doubts, and against all survival instincts he threw caution to the wind and bounded down the rocks, wagging his tail furiously.

The stranger stopped. He smiled. And then he laughed heartily. "Well, 'ol fella, look at you! I'll bet you're thirsty. Here," and stooping down, the man made a cone out of some paper and poured water into it. And Tobias drank. He would gladly have gone home with this man, given him his heart, stayed with him forever. But it was not to be.

The man stopped walking when Tobias began to follow him. He turned, directed Tobias to go from him. His whole demeanor changed and Tobias could sense that the man was burdened with problems of his own and had no room in his life for another soul, another problem. So Tobias stopped, and his tail drooped.

"Oh, don't worry," the man's voice gentled, "if I see you out here again, I'll have some food for you , maybe a sandwich."

Tobias, who knew the word "sandwich" very well, understood that the man with the backpack might return. He had been nearing a town when he had stopped to make this cave his home, and on several occasions he had seen a truck on the rutted road to his south.

But no one had come this close to him before.

Only this man had come. Only this man had been a friend.

It was several days before Tobias saw the man with the backpack again but this time he did not approach him. This time the man had a companion with him, and the companion had a rifle and walked with a purpose.

The accident that occurred that day, the sudden sound of panic from the men below, struck a deep fear into Tobias and sent him cowering back into his cave. When he emerged, his friend was gone and his friend's companion was running back to the road where he had left his truck.

When the man started his truck and drove away, Tobias crept down to the mine that the men had been exploring and he found the shaft into which his friend had fallen. He listened but there was no sound from the depths below. He whimpered; he pawed the dirt, circled and pawed at it again. Finally he lay down by the opening. This man had been a friend to him. He would keep watch.

Tobias did not move for several hours until he heard the truck return, and then he fled.

CHAPTER 5

"Well you can call it a shame if you want, what happened to that man Davis out at the mine, but I can tell you that I warned him more than once, told him that the ground was soft, too soft, could suck a man down in a minute.

"If you ask me it was that dog that lured him to his death. He thought I didn't see him standing up there in that cave watching me, but I saw him, all right."

Harold Pinehurst was a tough, sinewy 61 year-old. He lived alone in an old shack that his grandfather had built not far from a mine that was long defunct. According to Harold there was still silver in that mine and if the right investor came along, he could prove it.

But the truth was that Harold didn't trust mining and had no intention of reopening the mine he had inherited. Ground too unsteady, he had told the few locals whom he trusted. Opens up and swallows people.

So it was probably true that when Davis walked down the path to Harold's cabin looking for a guide, Harold warned him that it wasn't safe.

Nobody who knew Harold was about to blame him for the accident. The only reason he took his rifle and went out there in the first place was to look for the dog that Davis had seen.

Harold had heard about that dog – come out of Death Valley, living in the mines, creeping around those hills like a wolf, stalking anything that moved. Didn't sound like a normal dog to Harold. No sir. Sounded evil. Sounded like he came up straight from hell.

So hours after the accident, when Harold returned followed by a second vehicle his mind was less concerned with Davis and how they were going to get him out of that hole, and more concerned with finding that spying, evil dog.

Somebody ought to kill him and it might as well be Harold.

Tobias, from the safety of his cave, listened intently to the men below. Harold had led two county officers, one being the local sheriff, to the scene of the tragedy. This time the trucks left the road and crossed the desert floor directly to the mine, a distance of 180 yards as the crow flies, but a bit longer when forced by the terrain to make curves and detours on the way.

Once they had arrived, there was much calling back and forth between the men as they checked the area with Harold standing the farthest from the mine entrance while the others ventured as close as possible.

There was constant complaining from the second officer that calling for help was futile. Cell phone service from the mines was not only spotty but from this particular location it was nothing but a string of annoying static.

The sheriff entered the mouth of the mine and knelt close to the vertical shaft into which Davis had disappeared. He called out several times to Davis, listened, and then shook his head.

The other officer began checking for footprints around the mine. He took a measurement of Harold's footprint in order to eliminate it. While he was circling around the area he found Davis' backpack, shook out the contents and finding nothing significant threw the empty satchel into the sheriff's truck.

Darkness fell early as the two trucks drove back across the desert. It was still late winter and heavily clouded which added to the depressing atmosphere.

Harold, who was the last to leave, had kept his eyes on the cave where he had seen Tobias but he had made no move toward it.

He was also wise enough not to bring up the subject of the phantom dog he was determined to kill to these officers who were engaged in the serious gathering of scientific data. Harold's theory would have to wait until the practical side of their investigation was complete.

As silence returned, Tobias emerged from his cave, crept down the hill and resumed his watch.

Following is a recap of the attempted rescue:

Day 1

Dawn: The Sheriff returns followed by two other vehicles. The men unload ropes and other equipment and stand around drinking coffee. A jeep pulls up with two NDOW

(Nevada Department of Wildlife) young men who volunteer to go down the shaft but are told to wait for authorization.

Noon: The BLM (Bureau of Land Management) arrives. The men unroll several papers, ancient maps of the mine, and bend over them. The shaft is identified: 190 feet – a vertical drop. Two of the men begin testing the sides of the shaft. They lower a light into the depths of the shaft. Most of the original reinforcement is gone, rotted away. They attempt to lower a video camera, but need more rope to harness it safely.

Once more rope is located, the video camera is harnessed and again lowered carefully, only to have it jam between the remnants of some wood supports lodged into the wall at about 40 feet down. The camera is freed but no longer trusted to transmit a clear picture. Two men go for a replacement.

Meanwhile, the BLM sets up a tent – this will be their control center. Lights on poles. Ham radio. Right before sundown, the BLM officer makes contact with a mining company. He requests a rescue team.

Tobias watches from his cave. No one has noticed him. When he leaves, he moves like a shadow through the rocks and roots that hold the shelf of his elevated hiding place secure. He circles back, away from the lights, and when he returns all that is visible is a sliding shadow against the hillside, the silent phantom of someone's fears, hardly a reality worth noticing.

Day Two

Morning: Two experienced rescuers arrive and rappel down the shaft with difficulty while everyone else stands around. They make two attempts, come up covered with dirt and sweat, but cannot reach Davis.

Noon: The new video camera arrives and is lowered successfully by a third man who gets within ten yards of Davis; he does his best to secure the camera so that the top half of Davis can be seen. Up above, the men gather around excitedly. Davis is alive but badly injured. His mouth seems to move slightly but only the sound of his labored breathing is heard through the camera's attached mike.

Of most concern is the serious, perhaps critical, nature of his injuries. His body from the waist down is hidden, lodged between earth and rock making movement almost impossible.

Evening becomes night and the voices drone on. The sheriff leaves. Rescuers leave. BLM stays in the tent. Ham radio crackles. Camera is still working but by 9 p.m. Davis' breathing has become raspy and intermittent. He is not moving.

Day Three

Mid-morning: Sheriff, Harold and three other local men arrive. Rescuers are making a new attempt. Half way down, the sides of the shaft give way and almost crush the rescuers, burying them under pounds of falling rock and dirt. They fight their way back up, shaking their heads. "No way. Can't do it." One man's helmet is cracked.

The sheriff, along with the other officers present, assess the danger and decide that it's not worth risking another life to continue. No sound from Davis' breathing has been heard since midnight.

Noon. The decision is made to send for the preacher. Nothing more can be done. The camera is still aimed at Davis' chest. If no movement can be determined for 30 minutes, the time of death will be recorded as 2 p.m.

The camera is dutifully monitored by two men for 30 minutes. Then, after a long and dfficult struggle, it is brought to the surface, packaged and sent to the coroner.

Late afternoon. Several cars line up on the road. A young woman, with three small children beside her, begins the long walk to the mine. Next, an older man, stout, mid-sixties, emerges from a dusty black limousine, bible in hand. He follows the others.

The woman approaches the sheriff and identifies herself as Davis' sister. The man with the bible, who is identified simply as Pastor Paul, is told he has been called to give Davis a final blessing. Has Davis been pronounced dead? By whom?

Pastor Paul cannot get a clear answer; he is escorted to the mine entrance by Harold. Everyone gathers round.

As prayers are said for Davis, the children make him a little shrine; they tie together two sticks to make a cross and plant it by the entrance to the mine. Then, they gather some small stones and arrange them in a circle around the cross. Davis' sister watches in dismay. She is still not sure of what is actually happening.

As the service ends she addresses her concerns to the sheriff while the other men, in low tones, discuss what is next on the agenda. The mne must be sealed so no one else can fall into it. Davis' sister hears and is horrified.

Harold takes over and explains that an open shaft is officially a hazard and must be sealed by law. Davis' sister says no; what if her brother is still alive? Are they sure? How can they be absolutely sure?

Harold looks up and sees Tobias watching. He thinks fast, "See that dog? He's no real dog – look at him. Came right out of Death Valley. He's a killer dog. Know why he's watching?" Harold turns to Davis' frightened sister, "He wants your brother's soul – been after it since day one, left his paw marks at the shaft opening. Look here, see where he scratched?

"God knows what that son of Satan has in mind," Harold is saying. "I'm going to stop him right now. Watch…"

And that's how it happened – just like that. No one said a single word. And Harold took his rifle and went half way up the hill to Toby's cave. And Toby walked out. And Harold shot him.

CHAPTER 6

Tobias sensed the image of the girl, saw her dimly through the clouds that filled his eyes. It had been one week since the bullet from Harold's rifle had shattered his right shoulder and filled his body with a throbbing pain. That night he crept down from his cave and hid in a crevice between some rocks behind the hill where he had been shot. Occasionally a trickle of water would appear between the rocks but Tobias made no effort to reach it. For two days he never moved at all.

On the morning of the third day, Tobias opened his eyes. The man who had shot him had returned, climbed to the cave, and was kicking the dirt and cussing loudly as he searched for Tobias. Tobias didn't move; he closed his eyes, and the man left.

And then one day the girl came. He could hear her talking to someone and her voice seemed soft and familiar to Tobias so that he wasn't sure if she were real.

She and the other human had come on bicycles, walking them in from the road, across the dried earth, their tires crunching on the cracked gravel around the mine. They left their bikes at the mine entrance, by the little shrine that the children had made for Davis, and for a few minutes they stood quietly beside the shrine.

It was the girl's companion, the younger boy, who noticed footprints and followed them around behind some rocks to where the earth had been disturbed. The girl came up beside him. She saw some items on the ground and reached for one of them and carefully inspected it.

They decided to climb the hill to Toby's empty cave and when they reached it they stayed there talking in low tones until almost dark. Tobias was comforted by their voices but still he never moved. He fell asleep by his little trickle of water. And when he awoke, they were gone.

It took Tobias all the next day before he felt well enough to hobble up to his cave to scent around it and investigate. There was a sandwich wrapped in brown paper. At first he looked at it suspiciously. He circled it; cautiously he sniffed. Tobias straightened – it was for him. It was from his friend under the earth, and it was the girl with the soft voice who had brought it here for him.

Tobias stood very still in his cave with his sandwich on the ground before him. He sensed the girl; he could feel her kindness envelope him, relax him, even as he had felt the kindness of Davis. And something heavy began to lift, ever so slightly, from his heart.

During the next few days Tobias ate the sandwich in small bites, never taking much, guarding what was left between his paws as he slept. The pain had lessened now but he was very weak, too weak to hunt for food.

So he dreamed of the girl who had brought him the sandwich.

And Tobias stayed.

Until there she was – a slight figure on the distant road. She was alone, walking her bike under a threatening sky that hid the sun and made it difficult for Tobias to see. He stood. He would go to her. He would limp bravely down from his cave and out of the wasteland that had been his home. His once beautiful eyes, now clouded with cataracts – white like the sky was white – would not stop him.

He began to walk … 30 yards. He would move beside her as long ago the angel had moved beside him

60 yards. He would protect her as he had failed to protect Davis, as he had failed to protect the crumpled lump on the dark road by his home two years ago.

90 yards. For a moment he could see her more clearly. He trembled. The pain in his shoulder had traveled, enveloped his chest. It was huge. It was in his mouth, his jaw. And soon, it was also in his eyes, and his vision turned red with it.

But strangely, the pain didn't matter. He had made up his mind. Perhaps he could not save Davis who lay broken and silent under the earth, but what was left of his life he could give to the girl.

And then she turned and saw him. Tobias' heart surged. He began to trot, his injured leg dangling in front of him.

Mira stopped, put down her bike. He was close to her now. He lowered his head; perhaps he could lie down beside her to regain his strength. But he was very weak, and he stumbled. And then he went down, a bag of bones on the empty road – an angel himself, still having trouble with his strange disguise, still new to his mission on this place called earth.

And Mira knelt and her arms wrapped around him, and her face buried into his fur. She held him. She spoke of her sorrow, of the immense pain she had felt when she had lost him, of the great trust and courage he had shown to come to her today.

She told him that no matter how it may have seemed, she had never given up on him. Although, she whispered, she would understand if he had given up on her.

Then, in perfect silence, she asked with all her heart for one more chance – for both of them.

And her prayer was heard.

She was still there, on the dusty road with his mangled body in her arms, when the moon appeared between the clouds and her father pulled up to take them home. "Is it … is it…?" her father asked her, kneeling down beside the two of them.

"Yes," she answered. And the floodgates opened so that Tobias heard her sob and he looked up to see them looking down upon him in the moon's pale light. And his tail moved, and gave a little wag. "It's him," she whispered. "It's Toby."

CHAPTER 7

"Only thing I feel bad about, Father, is that I didn't kill that cursed dog the day I shot him. I don't pretend to be perfect but it's just plain wrong to leave some critter half dead out there. Desert's too harsh."

Harold was confessing to Monsignor Gene Cawley, the only person with whom he could discuss things like this for going on twenty years. Because Harold wasn't Catholic and never went to church, his confessions took place on a lawn chair outside his cabin, which was fine with Father Cawley who wasn't really a Monsignor.

"I got anxious – wanted to finish it quick." Harold looked over at the priest. "What if he bolted right past me? Terrible sight to see, him ravaging some little kid came to say good-bye to Davis." Harold sighed, "Got the dog in his shoulder, Father, close to his heart as I could."

Father Cawley looked down at his beads. He wore the simple cassock and sandals of a Franciscan. He knew that Harold wasn't finished so he just nodded and waited for the rest.

"Thing is – I can't find him. I went out to finish him off and he was gone. Rumor is he was seen in Creosite, dragging himself around that ghost town over there – scared some tourists, ran 'em back to their car.

"Sooner or later he'll kill somebody, Father. He might eat 'em too." Harold surveyed his own campfire pit across the yard, several small bones among the blackened wood chips. "Why are you smilin?" he turned back to the priest. "He's hungry, ain't he?" Harold snorted, "dogs eatin people ain't funny, Father."

"Why not let it be for awhile, Hal." Father Cawley studied his toes in the fading light. "If the dog is still alive, we'll hear. Tourists are always seeing things that aren't there. Give it time."

But Harold was in the grip of something far too powerful to ignore. So, aware of this, and spooked by it, he left his cabin two days later, and went looking for the Franciscan priest.

Father Gene, when he was in town, had use of a two room cottage right behind The Living Waters Baptist Church. It was a strange place for Harold to continue his confession but neither man seemed to notice.

"Fear come down and grabbed hold of me, Father. I know I have to kill that renegade mongrel soon, but every time I go out to look for him, something blocks me. Maybe he really is evil. Maybe Satan is protecting him for real. Is that possible, Father?"

Father Gene shook his head slowly. He was in his early seventies and had heard almost every excuse imaginable when someone was determined to avoid the truth. "You're just feeling guilty, Hal," he said quietly. "It's not only about the dog, and Satan's got nothing to do with it.

"Davis is dead," the priest continued. "When his time is

up, the dog will die too. You can't change any of it by going out there on your own like a madman. As I said before – let it be."

Harold, however, was just getting started. The way he saw it, Father Gene was right about one thing. Only a madman would go after Tobias alone. He needed a posse.

But Harold was smart as well as devious. The threat to local families of a mad dog roaming the hills wasn't enough. But if visitors learned of the danger, the town itself could suffer. So he'd start with the tourists.

Harold was grinning as he walked home that evening. It was early spring. The hikers and bikers would soon appear – small groups with their tents and trailers on their way upstate or over to Death Valley. These were usually city folk out for a desert adventure that was safe and predictable. Scare 'em and they'd run.

Harold stopped to review his sign. It was nailed to a post not far from the edge of town. There was an arrow, a WELCOME with the faded sketch of a bobcat encouraging tourists to leave the paved road and travel up the curving trail to his shack for an "amazing treat."

That treat, depending on the time of day, was often an invitation to share in the fixing and eating of Harold's rattlesnake supper. He would build a fire, sharpen his knife, and expertly skin a recently caught sidewinder while his visitors watched. He would slice the meat into long strips and roast them to a crisp. Then he would smack his lips and offer a taste all around, while sliding the meat into his mouth right from the blade of his knife.

Showing off for tourists was what Harold did best. But up until now it was mainly for fun. His routine went like this: First, he would show them a long line of animal skins hanging from a wire strung beneath the overhang of his cabin's roof. Then he would point to a 16 inch kangaroo rat that he had stuffed and placed in an upright position by his cabin door. "That's my guard rat," he would say, grinning. "Want to buy it?" This routine needed to be tightened.

So for the next few weeks, Harold stepped up his game. Right after "supper" and a quick look at the animal skins, he would pull his lawn chairs into a circle and invite his guests to join him for a "true tale that no one else has the nerve to tell."

He would sell them each an orange soda from his cooler and then proceed with his stories of the killer dog that never slept, the dog who came from the depths of hell and whom no amount of bullets could stop as he crept into homes and tents looking for prey.

As Harold's creative storytelling expanded, and his audience's horror grew, the satanic dog of the mines grew horns. Like the small triangular projections that protected the eyes of the sidewinder. the horns on Harold's imaginary dog could be lowered to cover his eyes and hide the evil in them. For the price of an orange soda, the tourists got their money's worth.

It seems that telling tall tales can become addictive. Harold was on a roll, and in spite of Father Gene's advice, he just couldn't stop.

Mornings found him at one of his favorite spots, a small plastic table outside the two-pump service station at the edge of town where tourists, as well as locals, would stop for a cup of coffee.

It was easy to target which type of camper was open to conversation. Harold would wave a friendly greeting, stand up and with a sweeping gesture offer to share his table. He warned of a wild dog, a killer dog that was hunting for people's pets, snatching them out of their tents, carrying them off in his mouth and shaking them until their coats slid clean off! And Harold had some of these skins hanging from a wire at his cabin to prove it!

Harold Pinehurst would talk about the dog from hell to anyone who would listen. But he never talked about Davis.

CHAPTER 8

When the sheriff arrived at the site of Jacob's camp, Tobias was resting in a lean-to that Jacob had built, safely sheltered by overgrowth, well behind the rest of the camp. The Amargosa River, which surfaced briefly here before resuming its ancient 180 mile underground journey, had formed a clear stream next to which the family – Jacob, his fourteen year-old daughter, Mira, and his twelve year old son, Benjamin, lived.

"Good day, Sir," the sheriff strode a few feet from his truck and stopped to survey the campsite. He stood with his legs slightly apart, one hand loosely on the handle of his holstered gun – a position not openly hostile, but obviously guarded.

Jacob, his son beside him, looked up from a table of herbs and seeds they had been sorting, creating labels as they worked. Jacob was in his early 40's, of slender build, his hair and beard a dark curly brown. Ben, minus the beard, was the same but younger of course, with piercing eyes and smooth dark skin.

"Been meaning to come out here and have a talk with

you," the sheriff continued. "Heard you might know something about a mad dog prowling these parts."

Jacob was silent.

"Dog could be rabid. Been seen foaming at the mouth. Snuck into some campers' tents, scared the hell out of 'em. My job is to keep people safe. Dog needs to be examined, possibly removed. Mind if I look around?" He began walking toward Jacob, moving to pass him and head into the brush.

"My daughter is back there," Jacob stood to intervene, "needs her privacy."

Mira was indeed "back there," having crawled into Tobias' hiding place with him, whispering to him that danger was near so he must stay quiet, although Tobias had lived in the wild long enough to know never to bark, danger or not, and would only on rare occasions allow a low rumble in his throat, usually as a warning.

It could honestly be said that from the first night they had brought him home, Mira lived in the lean-to with Toby, eating when he ate, and even bedding down with him at night. It was unnecessary and childish according to Jacob. But what could he do? It was love.

It had been close to a week since Tobias had fallen back, literally, into their lives. They had found a veterinary hospital willing to treat him that same night, driving over 100 miles down the western highway almost into California in order to reach it before it closed.

The doctors did their best but once they cut him open the bleeding was fierce and they had to stop and sew him back up before they had finished the job. His shoulder had been shattered into dozens of small bones, some of them mere splinters painfully imbedded in adjoining muscles. Tobias was much too weak for the lengthy surgery needed to remove them all.

"This will help with the pain," the family was told. "Keep him still, never mind what he wants to do; it's important that he move around as little as possible."

So they were given some pills and ushered out, carrying a limp Tobias in their arms. "Give him plenty of water when he wakes up," they were told at the door, "and bring him back in two or three weeks. We'll see if he's strong enough to continue."

Jacob was blocking the sheriff's path. "If you give us some warning, an hour or so, you're welcome to come back."

"I'm …what?" The sheriff looked genuinely incredulous. "This here is public land – case you didn't know. Far as this whole valley goes, and that includes the marshes and the up-land all the way back to the mountain, I don't need your wel-come. You can call your daughter out here or not, but I don't need permission – from you or anyone else, to search this camp."

He glanced toward Jacob's truck. "Now you listen to me," he continued. You come in from California and nobody bothered you. You're camping here for free, due to the kind-ness of our local citizens. You're using our river water free. From what I hear, your kids don't go to school and you may be hiding an animal that's diseased."

He paused, walked a few steps toward his truck, and then turned back. "Tell you what. I'm coming back here with two of my men in a few hours. We aim to search this site, and all the land around it, whether you like it or not. If you have a permit for what you're doing out here, I need to see it. If you have a dog, he needs to be restrained and I need to see proof that he's clean. If any person or animal makes a move toward my men, I'll kill 'em. Understand?"

Jacob nodded.

"All right, then." The sheriff reached his truck but stopped, looking back at the campsite. He remembered his pledge to treat all visitors with respect. "Nice place you got out here," he said grudgingly, "fixed up real nice." He opened the cab door. "You all have a nice day, now."

And he was gone.

CHAPTER 9

"Father, I'm wondering if Davis could be still alive." It had been almost three weeks since the mine had been sealed and this was the first time Harold had mentioned Davis to anyone. Father Cawley had just sat down on the frayed lawn chair beside him.

For a few moments, Harold was silent. Unburdening his soul, even to the good Father, was downright painful. But it had to be done. A man can lose his mind keeping too much covered up.

"I'm having dreams that I don't like," Harold spoke quietly but Father Gene could hear him clearly, "about Davis clawin his way up through all those rocks and dirt. I should have warmed him more 'n I did. I need forgiveness, Father."

"Just bow your head and ask for it, Hal. The Good Lord is merciful. It's too late now to worry about Davis. What's done is done."

"I know. I know. But what about that dog I shot? It's been more 'n two weeks; he should be dead by now, food for the scavengers. But where is he? Where's the damn body?"

Father Cawley didn't answer. His toes had been going

numb on him lately and he used occasions like this to wiggle them, get the circulation going.

Harold continued. He wasn't looking at Father Gene; they were sitting side by side with the cooler on the ground between them, an arrangement that made it easier for Harold to get to the point.

"I'll wager that little dark eyed girl is hiding him ... uh... huh … no wonder I can't find him … got him hidden down in the valley, along the river … that's right … plenty of brush where that family of hers is camping."

Father Cawley's eyes closed. Harold was intent upon rambling on about the dog. Fine, let him. But now he was bringing a child into it, and although Harold still wasn't making much sense, the priest was more alert than he appeared to be. Relaxed in the chair, his eyes closed – yes, but he was listening. Father Gene was always listening. Even when his head fell forward onto his chest and he appeared deep in slumber, he wasn't. He was listening.

Harold sighed. He reached into the cooler and pulled out an orange soda, glanced over at Father Gene's closed eyes, replaced it and took out a beer. He didn't open the beer; he rarely drank anything alcoholic. All the same he took comfort from it, holding it for a while and then putting it down on the ground beside his chair.

"You know," he said, "I could follow her if I wanted to," Harold's voice had a creepy edge to it. "I could prove she's hiding him. I almost did just that. But you know how people talk – might look like I had intentions on her, instead of the dog. Imagine, Father Gene, me runnin after a skinny little girl like that. Looks like she's about twelve."

Harold double-checked that the priest's eyes were still closed, "She's a sneaky one, though," he continued, "always lookin back over her shoulder – got one of them cell phones."

Harold was mumbling now, head down, so that Father Gene had to concentrate just to hear him. "She could be Middle Eastern, one of those terrorist types," he was saying. "Nobody ever seen her mother. Father looks Jewish; *supposed* to be Jewish. I've got my doubts though – doubts about him, doubts about all of them. Suppose he is Jewish, why would he bring his kids out here to the desert? I don't trust him. Not a lick. Not one lick. Not with the Test Site right over the hill."

Father Cawley sighed. He sat up and reached into the cooler for a soda. The ice had melted but the can was still cold. "Jacob is a scientist, Hal – a biologist. Government is trying to restore our land, bring back the natural habitat lost in the mining days. Not just anyone can do that kind of work – have to be checked out, have to show credentials."

Father Gene's eyes were open. He looked over at Harold. "How could a habitat biologist on a government contract be a terrorist?"

"Terrorists are smart, Father," Harold had to smile in spite of himself. "Slimy," he said, nodding his head for emphasis, "but smart."

Well, they needed a break after that. So they took one, Father Cawley making a trip to the outhouse while Harold relieved himself in the brush. Feeling better, back in their chairs as the air cooled and evening approached, they continued.

"Well, Harold, it's a beautiful night. The desert will be blooming soon. Best time of year, if you ask me." The

Franciscan sighed. "So don't you worry about our little visiting family camped out there in the valley. It's safe to say they're as American as we are."

Father Gene let a small smile escape him. "And you can relax about the Test Site. No one's going to breach that fence. Government has eyes, Hal. You'll just have to take this old priest's word for it."

"Maybe. But all the same, I'll be watching with them." Harold looked away. After a few moments he spoke again. "So ... tell me, why would these kids want to keep a diseased dog from his natural death?"

"Where's the proof that he's diseased?" Father Gene was beginning to lose patience. "Look, Harold, if these children are hiding the dog, it's to protect him. It's out of mercy, not because they want to give Harold Pinehurst a hard time. They're innocent kids, Hal." Father Gene softened his voice, "They help their father, and they say their prayers."

"They do, do they?" Harold's voice had changed again, making Father Gene take a second look at him. His face was drawn as he spoke; he looked older than he usually looked,

"Well, too much religion can be just as dangerous as not enough," he was saying. "No offence, Father, but that girl is aiding the devil by hiding that dog from those of us who rightfully want to kill him. She's acting like a fool, trying to prolong his miserable life, like she's thinks she's Joan of Ark."

"You mean Francis of Assisi," Father Gene corrected him gently. He leaned forward adjusting his earpiece. He wore one in each ear, sometimes allowing them to dangle while he spoke. "You mean Francis of Assisi, caring for the animals."

"No I don't. I mean Joan of Ark, riding her bike all through the desert. I saw her more than once after word got out about that dog, saw her leaving the road and following the trails into the mines like she's was going into battle, like she was looking to save a country not a dumb dog."

"It can't be wrong to care about other creatures, Harold." The priest spoke quietly but with a measured firmness in his voice that meant the conversation was over. He took a long breath, letting it out slowly, "You need to lighten up, my friend, before you give yourself a stroke."

But Harold didn't hear him. He was working on a new way to find Tobias.

Under normal circumstances, Father Gene was a patient man. He took things slow. "Give it some time," he liked to say. "Things will work out." But time was not on Toby's side and Father Gene knew it.

Guilt can be a wicked thing, he wrote in his journal later that evening, and the need to assuage it can torture a man and drive him to extremes. The Franciscan had known Harold for many years but never had seen him so obsessed. Following a child? No, this was wrong. Her family was as innocent as the dog they protected if, in fact, they were protecting him. Yet both were becoming targets.

To make matters worse, Harold had begun to gather a regular posse to search with him, men who would stop at nothing to find Tobias, men who sincerely believed it was their civic duty to hunt him down.

And now, the local news was reporting that the body of a hiker had been found mauled to death just north of town.

Speculation had it that although a mountain lion had been seen nearby, a band of coyotes led by a wild dog had performed the original attack.

Father Gene quietly took out a blank sheet of paper and began to draw. It was long and painstaking work, bending over the low light in his little room. Finally, he smiled, folded the paper, and turned off the light. The map he had drawn was perfect. *Just in case*, he said to himself. *Just in case.*

CHAPTER 10

"Do you know what they do?" Mira was sitting on the edge of Ben's bed. It was late but the light in their father's tent still burned. "They kill every wild animal in the area and then they chop off their feet and their heads and put them in a bag and take them to their lab to measure them against the marks on the dead person's body."

Ben was speechless.

"That's what they do," Mira paused. She looked at her brother with such an intense look that he shuddered. "That's what they'll do to Toby if they find him."

They won't find him; how could they find him, Ben wanted to say, but he couldn't say it. "What should we do?" he said instead.

"Oh Ben," Mira hugged her knees, rocking back and forth as she spoke, "I don't know. I don't know."

Because hiding Tobias was getting to be a problem. At first they had kept him close to home, moving him at first light into some thick brush along the river and then bringing him home by mid-morning. This was because the sheriff's visits were always early, hoping to catch the sleeping family by surprise. But soon the sheriff was joined by others and the sound of their high boots, moving up and down along the Amargosa, became common at all hours of the day.

There were also unexpected visitors, neighbors from nearby ranches, friendly tourists self-guiding on the birding paths and curious about their father's work. And now that Toby was feeling better he was becoming the sociable type, limping out of his shed in the homemade sling that Jacob had made for him to greet the visitors with wags and smiles.

So, by the middle of Toby's second week with the family, the children considered finding a safer hiding place for Toby.

They discovered a hidden arroyo not too far out in the valley where the Amargosa had recently begun to surface. New growth was springing up along both sides of the shallow ravine and bending over it protectively – a good cover for Tobias. But this idea was risky because Tobias didn't like being left alone and would only lie down and get comfortable if one of the children stayed with him. Tying him was out of the question because, as Ben explained when his father suggested it, Tobias would struggle to be free and could hurt himself.

But considering his injured shoulder, Jacob had argued, and with one leg in a sling, wouldn't Tobias need to rest after the long walk out there?

Why not leave him with his blanket and his rawhide bone for a few hours, as a test? If it worked, they'd have a safe alternative for hiding him. Best of all, a surprise visit by the sheriff would turn up nothing. Why not simply trust Toby – reassure him they'd be back, and tell him to stay?

"I don't think that would work, Dad," Mira countered, amazed that her father would even suggest such a thing, considering Tobias' history. Toby loved them, yes, but Toby was Toby.

"He's not a puppy, anymore," was all she would say. "He has a mind of his own."

She was right – it was true. So on the first day that they followed Jacob's suggestion with Ben actually using the dreaded word, "STAY," Toby sat down, watched them go and patiently assessed his situation.

Hadn't he been lonely long enough? Hadn't he "stayed" long enough? Although he relished the children's attention, when that wasn't available maybe he should take another look around – see what other company might be available.

Which is what he did. He simply limped out of his hiding place and looked around. He was looking for what he always looked for when he needed company – a warm body to lean against, a warm breath to comfort him. And he found it. He found dozens of soft warm bodies – not cattle exactly, but close enough. Desert burros.

Amazing. Wonderful. And so, in the way Tobias had that only other animals and a few select humans could see, Tobias smiled. Who would have guessed it? Friends.

At first they hardly knew what to make of him – these feral burros for whom the desert scrub, the hidden springs and rich variety of shrubs to nibble on, early flowering pepperbush and wolfberry, native bluegrass and wild rye, tender shoots of delicious barley, had been all theirs to thoroughly enjoy.

But as usual, Toby's whole demeanor, his absolute trust in their acceptance as he hobbled smiling into their midst, worked its charm. Yes, even wild burros have hearts that can melt.

And so Tobias spent a wonderful lazy afternoon among

the desert burros, the sun warming his coat, listening to them munch on all the emerging springtime grasses, moving along and munching with them, as happy as could be.

Mira found him a full half-mile from where they had left him, much closer to the road and an obvious curiosity to a busload of tourists who were lined up across the marshes looking at him through binoculars.

"I told you, Dad. We just can't leave Tobias alone. He might decide to go into town next time." It was later that night. Toby was limping badly after his burro excursion and it took forever to get him home.

"All right ... all right," Jacob was exasperated. "Keep him closer to home – take turns with him. You can bring him back before sunset, but for this next week you need to get him out of here by dawn. I'm expecting some students from the Conservancy and who knows when that Pinehurst fellow will be snooping around again.

"And, Mira," he continued, "no more sleeping in the shed with him." Jacob looked back at his work. He mumbled, "I wouldn't put it past Pinehurst to put a bullet through that shed if he knew Tobias was in there," which, whether he intended it or not, insured that wherever the children decided to hide Tobias, it wouldn't be in the camp shed.

"How about behind that old tailings dump where the mill used to be?" Mira brought up the idea that very night, sitting on the bottom of Ben's sleeping bag which like her own was six inches off the ground on a half inch 4x7 plywood board, braced with two-by-fours and set over ten cinder blocks. Jacob had brought two fold-up cots for them but the children much preferred their spacious platform beds with the cot mattresses on top and plenty of room for books and flashlights.

"Too far." Ben looked up. He had been leaning on one elbow, reading,

"But no one ever goes back there. It's off limits, and best of all it's full of sidewinders."

Ben was silent. "Why do you suppose it's off limits?" he said finally.

"Who even cares?" Mira gave him a disgusted look. "We went in there, remember? There's a hill in the back and an opening in the rocks – a perfect hiding place." She paused, "Nothing happened to us, did it?"

"It's too far for Toby; we'd have to pull him in the wagon. He'd hate it, Mira." Ben sighed. "And there are other things to consider."

"Like what?"

"Bats," Ben answered. "Dozens of them. Hundreds of them."

"But don't they sleep all day? They wouldn't bother Toby, Ben." Mira spoke quietly, looking down at the sleeping bag. "Toby would be safe in there with them – in his own cave. He could even stay in there at night," she stopped. "He used to have his own cave, remember?"

"Okay, we'll check it out." Ben yawned. "No one's going back into that dump to look for him, especially at night, that's for sure."

He paused, "Mira, what if the bats *are* a problem? Haven't they been sleeping all winter? They might be hungry enough to attack anyone – even us!"

Mira smiled, "So? Don't be so scary. They won't bother

us; but if a few of them do, and if they decide to dive at us, or at whoever else comes creeping around Toby's cave, so what?"

She paused, "At night, though, like you said, bats or not, he'll be safe.

They both were right. Although the men hunting for Toby might check around the dump in daylight hours simply as part of a wider search, night was a different story. Night belonged to the desert, not to man.

Neither crazy Harold Pinehurst, the sheriff, nor anyone else would wander out that far into the desert after dark to look for Tobias, opening the rusty iron gates, tripping over rocks, disturbing sidewinders and tarantulas and waving off the waking swarms of low flying bats.

The few times a nighttime search had been demanded for a lost hiker or reports of someone injured, the searchers could be seen for miles, the headlights of their 4x4's tilting left and right, their flashlights waving up and down as they constantly checked their pants and socks for spiders – especially the much feared brown recluse whose bite was known to release a venom so poisonous that even after a slow and painful recovery the poison could strike again a year later and reopen its path of frightening skin-scarring necrosis.

In other words, it was a hazard out there at night – the desert's way of protecting its own.

It might seem strange to think of Tobias, a domesticated dog with a scraggly coat and one leg in a sling, as one of the desert's adopted own. But strange or not, that's what he was.

CHAPTER 11

D o you think it's a safe place for him, Father Gene?"
It was two days after they had moved Tobias to his
cozy cave behind the dump, taking turns keeping
him company as Harold Pinehurst and his growing band
of vigilantes searched the surrounding hills for a killer
dog that did not exist.

It was Sunday morning. If time permitted before his
rounds, whenever Father Cawley was in town he held a
service for local Catholics in a small room at the Baptist
Church. This was not a complete mass like the one he
offered monthly, but it was still an opportunity to pray
quietly.

Mira was the first to arrive. She explained the hiding
place they had found for Tobias, up the hill, in the rocks
behind the tailings dump, but she was terribly concerned
that someone might find him.

"Well, yes, it sounds safe enough for a few days,"
Father Gene was preparing for the service. "Be sure the
entrance is blocked and watch that no one sees you go in
there." He smiled at Mira, "You love that dog, don't you?"

"Yes, I do. My dad doesn't understand." She paused, "Do you understand?"

Father Gene didn't answer. His kindness, however, was obvious to Mira so she took a risk and continued, "Father, can I ask a huge favor of you?"

"Of course. What is it?"

"Well, my mom grew up in a little village in Egypt. She told me all about it. The priest who came to her village would bring gifts for the children. He would walk around and bless each room in each home. Most of the homes, like my mom's, were small with only a few rooms but they always had one room on the side, attached to the house, for the animals. So when the priest blessed the people in their homes, he also blessed the animals in *their* homes."

"So you want me to go out to Tobias and bless him and bless his hiding place?"

"I do, Father. Oh, thank you. Thank you so much." And Mira did a little hopping dance, the one she used to do when she was small, with her hands behind her back, hopping back and forth from one foot to the other, smiling in anticipation of the blessing Toby would receive. Father Gene smiled too. She had won him over; he would bless Tobias. Toby, however, might need more than a blessing.

Father Cawley had a long day ahead of him before he could bless Tobias. In his capacity as a Franciscan priest, he traveled the several desert towns around Death Valley. It was Father Cawley who baptized and counseled, who prayed with the sick and who spent many hours listening to their problems and complaints.

He knew that Tobias was a growing concern to locals but

now the outlying communities were playing copycat, creating outlandish stories about the killer dog's relentless search for souls.

Another thought that was bothering Father Gene was his concern for Pastor Paul. He knew the Baptist preacher well and was sure that he too was being bombarded with questions about the "dog from hell."

But what had been haunting Paul, Father Gene guessed, was that when he had been called to conduct a funeral service for Davis, there had been no first-hand medical determination, no real proof, that Davis was dead. Yet with the pastor's blessing, right or wrong, Davis was assigned to his underground tomb.

To most observers, considering the extent of Davis' injuries, the fact that he was two thirds buried in dirt and rock – a new fall of which could completely bury his rescuers with him, the decision to call off the rescue seemed reasonable.

To Pastor Paul, however, none of that mattered. Without absolute proof of Davis' death, the nagging concern that he may have possibly endorsed a homicide was a burden no man of conscience should bear alone..

And finally, unknown to the unobservant, the Franciscan like his Order's patron saint had a deep affinity for animals, for all of nature including bugs and birds and all things growing, but especially for the suffering, the injured, the most innocent of creatures that crossed his path.

In other words, for those who believe in the pre-ordained, a case could be made that Tobias had come into his life for a very specific reason.

* * *

The road back into town was empty that Sunday evening and the Franciscan drove slowly. It had been a tedious day, exhausting not because of the demands upon his services but because, just as he had feared, at every stop there were new stories of the phantom dog who, bloody and foaming, was roaming the hills looking for souls.

As he had feared, The Devil of the Mojave was becoming a cult and nothing he had said had been able to stop it.

Traffic was sparse as he approached the barren desert area north of town. Checking to be sure he was not being followed, Father Gene turned off the road and followed a narrow trail that wound up into the hills and led him to a vast open area in the center of which a giant rocky pile of debris lay like a wounded animal.

He opened the rusty gate, drove slowly to the back of the dump and stopped. With only moonlight to guide him he made his way to Toby's cave. He was carrying water and a few rib bones wrapped in wax paper that a grateful family had given him.

Tobias' ears went up, and he struggled to stand as he heard the sandaled feet approach. A wave of relief engulfed him as a gentle hand reached out to stroke his fur and to inspect the injured shoulder and the homemade sling that held his damaged leg in place.

Father Gene sighed deeply. The healing was slow. Although Tobias was safe and cool, although his burs and ticks were gone and his appetite, at least for ribs, was coming back, the pain when he stood was in his eyes. He could not run. There was no way that he could save himself should he be found.

As Father Gene emerged back onto the paved road he noticed something that he hadn't seen before: Harold's truck, parked a distance away, next to a small settlement, under some cottonwood trees.

CHAPTER 12

"Ben, I'm scared."

It was early Monday, the day after Father Gene's visit to Toby. Mira had come over to Ben's platform bed and positioned herself once more on the foot of his sleeping bag. She tucked her feet under her thighs so that she was sitting cross-legged.

Ben was sleepy, "What?" He squinted, propping himself up into a half-sitting position.

"Someone followed me, just now, when I took my bike to check on Toby. So I circled back and came home."

Ben lifted his head. For a moment he considered what she had said, "Did you see who it was?"

"No." Mira clenched her knees, "Will *you* check on him for me? There's a jug of water for him in the yard." She began rocking back and forth with nervousness, "Just be really careful. Okay?"

Ben nodded. He paused, "Wow, you were followed? For sure?"

"I'm sure. But don't tell Dad. I think maybe we should have a gun. Can you find us one, a pellet gun maybe … for protection."

Ben was in shock. Was this really happening?

"Or maybe mace," Mira looked toward the yard. "I couldn't tell if it was a grown man or a boy who was following me. But it was human."

Ben sat up, fully awake. "You have to tell Dad. You have to, Mira. It's serious."

"I know. I will. But will you see about the gun first? Dad's not up yet," she opened the tent flap and looked over at her father's tent. "Maybe check at the store, okay?"

"Yeah - okay. Go on, Mira. Let me get dressed."

Ben scrambled out of his sleeping bag, pulled on some clothes and went outside to get his bike. "Don't worry," he said to his sister, who was watching him from across the yard. "I'll check on Toby and be right back."

"We need a gun, Dad." It was mid-morning. Jacob, his second cup of coffee in a tin cup, was standing at the camp stove frying some eggs. Ben stood beside him, shoulders back, looking as tall as possible. He had just returned on his bike from the town's only market. On the cork notice board outside the store there was a posting for a pellet gun: Good condition. $35.

Ben handed his father one of the camp's tin plates and watched as Jacob slid two fried eggs on to it. He tried to catch his father's eye, "I've been to Toby. None of us should go to him without a pellet gun at least. It's just common sense, Dad. It's dangerous out there; sidewinders are everywhere."

Jacob looked up, "You don't need a gun, Ben. No." He turned back to the stove, "No killing the wildlife."

"Then you need to keep Mira home." Ben lowered his

voice. He was standing almost shoulder to shoulder with his father and the urgent tone in his voice made Jacob's eyes narrow.

Jacob's cooking slowed as, without turning, he gave his full attention to his son.

Ben continued, "Do you think the men who want Tobias aren't watching her, following her? I'll take over, but I need a gun."

"All right, what's going on here?" Jacob turned off the stove and faced the open tent. Mira was at the table, head down, scraping her plate. "Mira, come here."

Jacob sighed. He waited.

The children stood before him, "Look," he spoke gently, "I know you've both been working hard to keep Tobias safe. It's been a challenge for all of us but in a few days he goes back to the hospital. Once they put him under and clean out his shoulder …" Jacob hesitated. The children's horrified expressions were obvious.

"Now what?" Jacob raised his voice. "They do this kind of thing all the time. It's nothing." He continued, "They can even fix him up with a metal plate to replace the bone."

"I don't trust it, Dad," Mira interrupted. "Can't we let Nature heal him?"

Jacob looked steadily down at his daughter. "No, we can't. But never mind that. Is someone following you, Mira? I need to know. Answer me."

"I'm not sure," Mira looked down. "It could be just one of the kids from town. They like to make fun of me because I'm Arab. They think all Arabs are Muslim. I just say, so what? So what if I'm Muslim? What's wrong with that?"

"Don't you explain that you're Christian?" Jacob looked worried. "It would be easier on you than defending Muslims."

"Mira doesn't care about 'easy'," Ben spoke up. "She's like you, Dad."

"But, anyway," Mira brought the conversation back on track, "Ben's right that Toby's not safe out there." She was persisting as only Mira knew how to persist. "He's getting stronger but he can't run yet. And by the way, how do we know that the veterinarians are right? Why didn't they give him a brace for his shoulder? And what about his poor leg? Why tell us to come back when he's stronger?"

"Maybe they plan to amputate it." Ben looked at Mira.

"They're not going to amputate anything," Jacob wiped his hands on a towel and walked several feet to his phone. He turned back to the children. "Toby's appointment is for Friday – that's in four days. I've made arrangements to board him there after his surgery. They're full now but from Friday on they have plenty of room – that's why we have to wait."

Jacob sighed again. He sat down heavily at his workbench and assessed the dozens of pods and leaves, seeds, and long silky fronds that would consume the rest of his day. They're so beautiful and yet they are threatened, he was thinking, replaced by man's ignorance with plants that were never intended to flourish here, plants that drink the precious water that these native plants and grasses need.

Ben looked at Mira. Their father was drifting into work-mode. Work-mode meant no more talk about Tobias. "In a few days," Jacob was saying quietly, "thank God, this will be all over."

"Ok, but until then, he's coming home." Ben paused;

he wanted to make sure his father heard him. "Even Father Gene agrees. Toby's not safe where he is. He needs to come home."

Jacob looked up. "Father Gene?"

Ben ignored the question and kept going. He was learning the persistence thing fast. "Tobias is our dog," he continued. "Forget everything else, Dad. Just do your work. Mira and I will defend our dog."

Ben looked over at Mira for support. "Let's go get him – are you ready?"

Two hours later Tobias came home, in a wheelbarrow, under a tarp. Ben stayed with him while Jacob and Mira went looking for Father Gene.

* * *

"Why do I have to come with you, Dad?" Mira dragged along reluctantly. "I want to stay with Toby. What if the sheriff comes again?"

"Ben will hide him." Jacob motioned her into the truck, gave the camp a quick once-over look and reversed out of it. "But we're going to need another place soon. Ever since that hiker was killed the sheriff and his men are out for blood. They'll take Tobias from us and nothing we can say will stop them."

Jacob stopped suddenly and turned to Mira. "You're with me because … because I can't have you being followed by these men, or watched. Ben is right; you're too …" But he stopped. It seemed inappropriate to continue. His daughter had no idea she was … well … pretty. She was expecting him to say 'naïve.' Either way, better to zip it, as Ben would say.

In a few minutes they were on the road to town, a quiet narrow road that ran parallel to the highway.

"From now on, you stay with me," Jacob glanced over at his daughter who was riding shotgun with him in the truck. She seemed so small, smaller than he usually thought her to be. "Got it?" he said in his don't-mess-with-me voice.

"You weren't so worried about Mom," Mira spoke with her head down. "People followed her too. Did you even try to understand why she left? Do you even check the news on the internet?"

The Living Waters was in sight. "We're not going to discuss that now, Mira," Jacob turned into the wide drive and edged around to the two cottages behind the main building. "This is about Tobias."

He parked the truck and turned off the ignition. "And I *do* worry about your mother."

Jacob slid out of the truck, "Now stay here and keep the doors locked."

The reason he had decided to keep Mira close was that, in Jacob's mind, she was as much of a problem as Tobias; he needed help with both of them. As a single Jewish father with no rabbinical counsel available, Jacob reasoned that Father Gene would have to do.

We are all children of the same Father, he had told Mira. Yes, yes, we argue just like you children argue. Muslims, Christians, and Jews. Everyone wants to be his Father's favorite. Sibling rivalry. It's normal. But we're all brothers who love and depend upon the same God. And deep in our hearts, we know it.

* * *

"I'm hoping you can help me, Father." Jacob sat down on the narrow porch's only chair to which Father Gene had directed him.

"Yes, of course, I've been expecting you, Jacob." Father Gene retrieved his other kitchen chair and pulled it out onto the porch, the screen door slamming behind him. He glanced toward Jacob's truck. Mira had lowered the glass half way for air and was sitting quietly.

"Did Ben tell you I stopped him today?" The priest sat down, facing Jacob, "That Pinehurst fellow could have spotted me last night. I brought some rib bones to Tobias."

Jacob shook his head slowly. "No, he never mentioned it – just that you knew where Tobias was and that you said it wasn't safe."

"So where is the dog now?" Father Gene was listening carefully.

"He and Mira brought him home. They just made the decision and did it. I don't know how to control them, Father; they have their own opinions about everything.

"Their mother's family is from Egypt but they were living in Palestine when all the political trouble started. I feel maybe my being Jewish … "

"No, no," Father Gene interrupted, smiling. "Children of all faiths, of mixed faiths, and of no faith at all, famously believe that adults misunderstand them. Finding their own solutions is nature's way, a practice run for when they will be on their own."

"But this crisis in the Middle East – the children's mother is there; she's been missing for over two years. And now … this thing with the dog." Jacob sighed deeply. "Ben tells me

Mira is being followed – followed! Father, she's fourteen! I feel … I feel …"

"Ah, yes, you feel threatened from all sides." Father Gene looked at Jacob. "Let's talk about the dog for a minute."

Jacob looked down, "That's just it. I don't know where in the world to hide him, Father. On Friday I have a place for him, but if he's discovered with us before then, the sheriff will take him from us for sure.

Jacob's voice was soft but betrayed the anguish that he felt, "Father, if Tobias is killed, I could lose Mira for good. I don't know what she might do." He paused, "She never forgave me for making her give him away."

Father Gene nodded slowly.

"We left him with strangers on the coast when we moved down to Los Angeles." Jacob paused again. "I had no idea she'd miss him so much. It's been almost three years now. And … here he is."

Father Gene studied his feet. "I see. I see." He took a moment to absorb the full impact of this new information.

So Tobias came all this way alone, he was thinking, *after almost three years. Why?* Finally, he spoke, "All right, I'm going to help you." The Franciscan took a folded piece of paper from his pocket.

"I planned on giving this to you today," he said. "Tobias should be safe here, at least for awhile." He reached out and gave the map to Jacob.

"But you need to understand," the priest continued, "that you don't have much time."

"Even when the current hunt by the sheriff is over, the

first time you're not looking Harold Pinehurst will move in on your campsite to finish the job he started."

Jacob stood, extending his hand to the priest. Father Gene looked directly into his eyes. "There may be more to this than meets the eye, Jacob. "Tobias came a long way to find Mira." he spoke quietly. "It's quite a coincidence, don't you think?"

The Franciscan paused. He looked past Jacob to the truck where Mira sat quietly. "Don't worry, Jacob," he said quietly. "Of course you need to keep Mira safe – that's a father's job. But, Jacob, the time may come when you should listen to her too."

CHAPTER 13

"Ben, Mira, come here, listen closely. We have a place for Tobias until the hospital can take him." Jacob was standing beside his truck with two empty five-gallon buckets "Fill these, Ben. Mira, get some extra blankets and then come back. Wait – check on Tobias. How is he?"

It didn't take long. The children gathered close to Jacob. "All right," Jacob reached inside his jacket and took out a folded piece of paper. "Father Gene knows of a cabin where the dog will be safe for a few days. It's ten miles northeast of here, back by the mountain, completely hidden. Hunters used it once, but no more."

"They're on to us, aren't they?" Ben spoke. "I was right. They're coming for Tobias now, tonight, aren't they?"

"I don't know, but soon. Father Gene thinks very soon. Here … look …" Jacob's hand was shaking as he unfolded the paper to show a pencil-drawn map.

Mira looked at his hand in amazement. She had never seen her father's hand tremble. She rarely saw any emotion in him. She was shocked. She stared. She had never guessed that he cared that much.

Jacob looked down at his daughter. He had struggled many times to tell her how much she meant to him. But now, he didn't have to tell her anything.

Heading northeast, mid-afternoon in Jacob's truck, bumping along off-road, following the rutted gullies into the desolate hills that rose from the valley floor to the mountain's edge. Finally, they slowed. The trail they were following had become impassable.

For some time an almost invisible wire fence had run parallel to their path. Now as they stopped it stood imposingly before them, a weathered sign warning any would-be visitors.

RESRICTED ACCESS. TOLICHA MOUNTAIN ELECTRONIC COMBAT RANGE – arm of the dreaded Nuclear Test Site.

It was a barren place and Mira shivered as she held Tobias on the seat of the cab, his head on her lap. Ben who had been riding in the back, scrunched among the supplies, studied the slight slosh of water in the buckets under his care. But the dreariness of the place did not escape him. The cabin Father Gene had drawn on the map with an X was only yards away from the fence.

Jacob sat silent, surveying the area. He too was having doubts. Although testing at the site had been suspended, it was here that the Amargosa, the generous source of so much life, began its journey.

For thousands of years it had drained here, moving in hidden channels beneath the earth, crossing the state and descending into Death Valley, appearing briefly between reeds and rushes, forming pools of clear water where wildlife could come to drink, and where wildflowers could grow tall and bend in the wind along its banks. Yet weapons testing, and the traces of death it left behind, cared nothing for this. *How many species,* Jacob was thinking, *could be at risk from what has happened here?*

"Let's go, Dad," Ben tapped on the glass between the cab and the truck's bed. Mira slid from under Tobias and helped him to the ground. The cabin was a one-room structure, un-locked, with scraps of faded notices attached to the door. Supplies were unloaded and brought inside. Tobias was led from the truck, walking reluctantly beside Mira.

"I don't trust this door, Dad," Ben stood by the door. One of the hinges was loose; he tried tightening it with a pocket-knife. "Ok, it's holding now, but Toby is smart. Confinement is a challenge to him – you know that. Let me stay with him."

Mira joined in, "We can both stay. There's plenty of blan-kets and water. Please, Dad?"

Of course they both knew what their father would say, so Jacob felt no need to answer. He simply looked at them, ushered them out the door and into the truck, and turned on the ignition.

"We'll be back in two days," Jacob was resolute as they started for home. "I'll stop by the bank tomorrow and we can begin to close up the camp and secure our things.

"We can drive him down to Edison on Wednesday, ex-plain that it's an emergency and see if they can take him ear-ly. If that doesn't work, we'll wait. We'll keep him with us, and wait right there until Friday.

"The point is … " Jacob's forehead was furrowed and his jaw was set, "the point is, we have options." It sounded good but no one looked convinced.

The rest of the ride was silent. Nobody liked leaving Toby alone such a long way from home, even for a day. At first they had pinned their hopes on finding a sanctuary. A sanctuary that harbored desert animals, even injured reptiles or birds, might understand and agree to harbor Tobias, at least for the rest of the week. Also, a sanctuary would not pre-judge.

But there were no sanctuaries. For 60 miles to the north and to the east, there was nothing. And to the west ... Death Valley.

There was one mid-sized town before Edison on the route south to the hospital, but they also knew about Tobias and had even published a sketch of him, (making him look as evil and as bloodthirsty as they could) in their local newspaper. There was a county animal shelter there that offered boarding but should they accept Tobias without realizing who he was, they would still be obligated to give a report of his injuries to county authorities. Most frightening of all, should they recognize him or determine for any other reason that he posed a threat, they could kill him.

Mira, however, had an idea of her own. She had told no one, not even Ben. This was because she wanted to have it all worked out before she presented it. Now she could wait no longer.

"I found the solution, Dad. For Toby."

The rest of the day had been quiet with Mira lost in thought and Ben helping Jacob with his latest project. The family was sitting down to supper. "It's completely safe," Mira continued, "and actually, it's ... perfect!"

Jacob glanced at her suspiciously.

"I have some new friends. They're staying in Arizona,

and we're invited to stay with them for the summer – Toby and me, both of us." Mira lowered her voice and her eyes, trying to prepare for her father's response.

"Who are these people? When did you meet them? And where?" Jacob shook his head. God help me, he prayed silently.

"I met them online. We've been communicating."

"Mira, no. You don't know them at all. After Toby recovers from his surgery, I'll drive him back to California where there are people we can trust, people who know us – real friends."

"These people can be trusted too." Mira's voice was soft, so soft her father and Ben had to lean in to hear her. "They work for peace all over the world, especially in Palestine, in the Middle East where Mom is.

"They believe all killing is wrong – even killing rebels and murderers. I told them Tobias was being hunted as a killer and they said it didn't matter. They said no one is irredeemable."

Mira took a breath, "That's what our Pope says too. That's what he always says … but" she had begun to stutter, "but … most people don't listen."

Jacob looked carefully at his daughter, "Well, they certainly do sound like good people. It's just that …"

Feeling encouraged, Mira continued. "How can you do your work and get paid if you have to keep driving around and worrying about Toby?" She looked up. "Arizona's not far – I'll have my cell phone and you can call me anytime. They have first aid stations over there. And I could bring my school books." She paused, smiling. "They live in tents, just like we do."

"That's what I thought. They're peace activists, Mira. The police might break up their encampments at any time. I know you admire them. I know one of the computers at our little library should have your name on it. But this idea isn't safe. I don't trust it – not for Toby, not for you.

"Mira," Jacob continued patiently, "Try to understand. How can I let you go anywhere with strangers? You're not even fifteen yet. I lost your mother to strangers. I can't lose you too."

"I'm *almost* fifteen." A flicker of anger crossed Mira's face. "And you didn't lose anyone; how can you say that? Mom went back to help her family. Remember? They were trying to get papers, so they could come here and be safe. Why don't you have faith in us, instead of always imagining the worst."

She took a breath, "Okay, here's the deal. Toby should go to Arizona even if I can't go with him. It would give him a chance to heal naturally. He can walk much better now; he's more balanced and sure of himself. Maybe he just needs more time."

Mira looked up at her father. "And like you said, these are good people. Toby would be safe with them – safer than he is here. Nobody would hurt him over there. Nobody would *want* to hurt him."

The room was silent. Jacob and Ben continued to stare at Mira and Mira just looked down at the table. For a few moments no one knew what to say. Finally she continued.

"They can pick him up wherever you say. It's up to you, Dad." Mira faltered. She could see where this was going but she bravely persisted, "All they need is for you to say yes." Tears were coming. Mira looked down, "You can call them whatever you want to. But to me and Toby, they're friends."

Mira stood, stopping the tears and continuing with a resolve that welled up inside her slight frame, a surprise to all of them. "But *I should* go with them, for Toby's sake, so he isn't scared. Maybe I'll go later, on the bus.

"After your work is finished in October," she continued calmly, reaching to collect the dishes, "we can all go home to California together. Maybe you can rent a house with a yard this time, by the mountains where it's cool."

"Mira, I said no."

"It's a new world, Dad," Ben spoke up. "And you know Mira. Or at least you should." He went to his father and placed his hand on the older man's shoulder, "We'd better get Tobias out of his hideout and down to that hospital fast. Or forget it, they'll both be gone."

But it was too late. Harold Pinehurst, the sheriff, and half a dozen men from the area were not to be outdone. The dog was nowhere in the valley where Jacob and his family were camped – of this they were confident. A few of his hideouts, one as recently as yesterday, had been found but he was in none of them.

Time to double down on following those kids, and time to take a real close look at their scientist father.

So on the morning the family was going back for Tobias, Harold Pinehurst was on watch sitting at his favorite plastic table outside the two-pump service station at the edge of town. He saw Jacob's truck come in, fill up with gas, and make the turn north onto the newly paved highway; with him were both kids but no dog that could be seen.

Harold went inside and called the sheriff. In less than four minutes the posse was ready to go. With an empty road and ten mile visibility they would be able to see Jacob's truck from a safe distance.

Not only were these men determined to locate Tobias and to kill him, they agreed with the sheriff's decision to charge Jacob with hindering an official investigation. He was a quiet man and seemed friendly enough but looks could be deceiving.

Of course the investigation into his scientific activities might come to nothing, but all the same, the sooner the town was rid of this family, the better.

But Fate intervened. Not only did Harold, the sheriff and his posse of hunters, follow Jacob in vain. Jacob never did pick up Tobias – that day, or any day.

No one did. Because when Jacob and the children arrived at the cabin, the door was laying flat on the ground, pushed open from the inside, one hinge ripped off. And Tobias was gone.

If circumstances were different, it might even seem comical – Jacob and the children racing back across the desert toward home (because where else would Tobias go?) while the sheriff and his convoy of trucks raced past them in the opposite direction, still hoping to find Tobias where Tobias obviously wasn't..

CHAPTER 14

"Do you think he can survive out here, Dad? Do you think he's strong enough?" Mira and her father were camped by a grove of cottonwood, five miles northeast of their campsite. They had been combing the desert uplands, the hills and dried out marshes for almost a week.

They had found two separate groups of wild burros and followed them patiently. They had followed the fence that marked the test site boundary and explored the huge crater at the foot of the mountain that rose ten miles behind their valley home.

"Of course he can," Jacob stirred the ashes of their fire to make sure no sparks remained. He began covering the ashes with surrounding sand. "Mira, Tobias is no ordinary dog. He crossed the Mojave. It's possible he needs the emptiness, the wild. Maybe he needs the open spaces to keep his heart calm, and the sky above him so he can to heal."

For a moment he was silent. When he spoke again it was with a kindness in his voice that seemed new to Mira, "You didn't tell your friends in Arizona where he was, did you?"

"No," she shook her head. "I wish now that I did." She glanced up at him. "I miss him so much, Dad."

Jacob nodded. "I know." After a moment he spoke again, "Tobias loves you deeply, Mira. Not coming home doesn't mean he doesn't love you."

"Like mom."

Jacob's breath caught. Had he heard right? He looked at Mira in the deepening dusk. Father Gene had startled him days ago when Jacob had expressed his fears for Mira, her obsession with finding Tobias, her unwillingness to accept the fact that he, like her mother, might never return.

"She hasn't got a clue, Father," he had said to the priest, "about the real world, about how treacherous and unforgiving it can be. Ben is much more practical. I think that Mira's just too innocent … you know, to see the whole picture."

Father Gene had let out a long breath. "What *is* the whole picture, Jacob," he had said, smiling slightly but looking directly into Jacob's eyes. "Do we know?" Jacob remembered suddenly the words of Father Gene that day at his cottage with Mira sitting in the truck. "Jacob, my friend," he had said, referring to the possibility that Tobias' search for Mira was for a reason that had nothing to do with coincidence.

"Of course you should protect her; that's a father's job," he had said. "But Jacob, the time may come when you should listen to her too."

So now, in the falling darkness of the desert night, Jacob listened to Mira.

"Mom is missing too. But it doesn't mean she doesn't love us. It's only been two years and, remember, she's been very busy. She could be on the way, looking for us right now.

It took Toby almost three years to find us. But he did it, didn't he?

"Mom will find us someday, Dad – just like Tobias found us." And Mira smiled. "I think they're two of a kind, not afraid of anything, just going out there on their own to do what they feel is right."

And then she smiled again, a warm smile that made her father smile too, "So naturally God knows this," she continued. "That's why He's watching over both of them."

"That's all well and good," Ben told her later that night, hoping to balance his sister's conviction of God's personal interest in their lives with what he saw as a healthy dose of common sense, "but maybe God likes to watch and see what we'll do on our own. Maybe there's a starving mountain lion out there stalking Tobias who means just as much to God as Tobias does."

"You can be really mean sometimes, Ben. Why don't you just leave me alone?"

"Because you're being stupid and expecting miracles and I don't think it's right. Maybe Mom doesn't want to come home. Maybe she's happy in Egypt. Or in Lebanon, with her relatives. Why can't you admit that?"

"I didn't say she was coming home right now," Mira flung back at her brother. "I said she *might* be coming home right now. Why do you want to torture me, Ben?"

But it was getting more and more difficult for poor Mira. Sightings of animal remains were frequent, especially in the hills to the west of town. Several hunters had come upon a recent cougar kill that resembled Tobias, and a small settlement over in Death Valley had reported that a large wolflike dog had been found dying from thirst ten miles north of Furnace Creek.

The dog was a skeleton, dried up, all bones and dirt, his mouth gaping open, eyes fixed and vacant. The hikers who found him did their best to revive him but in spite of their patience, their massaging fingers, wet towels and compresses, he was unable to swallow, tongue swollen huge and purple, throat locked up against even a drop of water. The only merciful thing to do was to end it for him, release him, let him go.

Strangely, however, as the weeks passed and as more reports of a dead Tobias surfaced, no one who had actually known Tobias believed them. Not Mira. Not Ben. Not Jacob. Not Father Gene; not even Harold Pinehurst. It made no sense; of course the dog should be dead by now. But they didn't believe it – none of them. They just didn't.

Until finally, after so much time had passed with no sign at all, not even a trace of Tobias, their faith began, ever so slightly, to waver. Which is why Mira's dream took on such strange significance.

He came at night. The family was accustomed to visits from wild creatures while they slept. The shadow of a coyote or a bobcat moving through the campsite was nothing to fear. Like graceful phantoms they would soon be gone, sliding back into the silence of the desert brush.

That was the difference; they never stayed. They never stood at the entry flap to the children's tent and waited – just waited. They never walked around the outside of the tent to the place closest to Mira and then lay quietly, almost invisible against the canvas.

Of course that didn't mean that one of them couldn't do this – lured by a particular scent, hoping for a scrap of food that missed the compost pile.

Even so, it wouldn't be Tobias. It couldn't possibly be Tobias. If he were still alive, he was far away, struggling to survive in the hills to the north, a lonely pariah seeking final refuge in the caves and mines that once had been his home.

But gone – definitely gone. Gone from those who wanted to kill him, and gone from those who wanted to save him. Gone from all of them. His story finished.

But maybe not.

"I'm going to tell Father Gene," Mira was busy getting her backpack supplied for the ride to town. "It's been two days now since Tobias came to me. I think Father Gene should know. I'm going to look for him."

"All right, but be careful," Jacob looked over at his daughter. His voice was quiet.

"Dad … did you see the blood?"

Jacob nodded. "I know it could have been from any animal, but in my dream he was hurting. And skinny. His bones stuck out of him like when we found him at the mine. Remember?"

Again, Jacob nodded.

"He wouldn't stay. He drank some water. I begged him to stay, but he wouldn't." Suddenly Mira stopped what she was doing and looked up at her father, "He hasn't come back. Maybe he's never coming back."

"Mira," Jacob moved toward her. "Here …" he enfolded her in his arms. "It's okay. He's alive, isn't he? In the dream he was alive. So even if that's all it really was – a dream, it's good. It's good news, Mira."

"You're right." Mira backed up. She smiled. "That's what matters – that he's still alive."

She was moving her bike out onto the gravel path when she turned back toward her father. "He tried to play with me, Dad. You know how he shakes his head and tries to dance?"

Jacob nodded slowly. Mira's words wrenched at his heart. "As hurt as he was," she continued, "even with his bad leg, he tried to dance."

CHAPTER 15

"Well, well, I had a feeling you'd be here." Father Gene sat down slowly next to Tobias on the floor of his cave. His fingers traced the dark red dirt where almost four months ago, the dog had been shot. Tenderly he pulled open the scraps of shredded bandage on the dog's shoulder, removed a blackened, blood soaked piece of gauze and swabbed the wound with alcohol. Tobias never moved.

"Still like rib bones? I'm going to bring you some."

The Franciscan moved his hand slowly through Tobias' coat. "Now what is this?" Gently he loosened a tuft of hair under the dog's belly. It was coarse, a light buff color but warmer, almost orange – like the sun.

"I see," he said softly, "you have a friend now, someone to keep you company, someone to keep the nightmares away."

For a moment Father Gene studied Tobias. "Maybe she came for you that night you were alone. Maybe she called to you." He looked into Toby's eyes and laughed softly.

"She's close by, isn't she?" he said after another moment of silence. "That's good, Tobias. That's as it should be."

Father Gene looked out across the parched land. It was twilight. Toby's sling was gone but he held his leg carefully, leaning with perfect trust against the priest, keeping most of his weight off of it. The bones seemed straight; if there had been a fracture, no sign of it remained.

"Now you just be patient," Father Gene spoke in a low voice, covering the old wound with a fresh bandage. It did not look good; the thin layer of fresh skin had been ripped open and the tissue beneath was raw and swollen. Infection. Even worse, the infection wasn't new. It had been slowly draining for some time, seeping out of the wound from deep inside, its rank odor signaling a growing danger.

"It hurts, doesn't it?" Father Gene looked up at Tobias. The dog's weight pressed against him. "You need some serious help, old boy," he continued. "All I can do is clean you up. It's not enough … it's not enough."

A moment later he paused in his work. He looked around. "If I could just get you out of here, Tobias. No doctor is going to crawl in here to fix you up." The priest sighed deeply. "But you won't come out. You won't move an inch from this cave, will you? Not for me, not for anyone."

For a moment more he studied Tobias, "That's it – isn't it? That's why you came back. You're convinced you have a job to do – right here. And even if it kills you, you're going to do it."

Father Gene stood, extracting himself carefully from the injured dog, brushing the dirt from his cassock and then turning once more to Tobias.

"Just so you know, Tobias," the priest smiled, his voice barely a whisper, "whatever happens, I'm on your side.

"And that's a promise," he added, moving toward the mouth of the cave and then, with resolute steps, continuing down the steep grade, past Davis' tomb, and into the night.

CHAPTER 16

"I know where he is, Gene." Pastor Paul Billings stood in the sun in front of his church. His Sunday service had gone well and he was smiling as his final few parishioners got into their trucks or moved into the morning haze on foot. The monthly mass for Catholics, officiated by Father Cawley was not scheduled to begin for 30 minutes, giving the two men time to talk.

"If you do, you best stay quiet about it, Paul." Father Cawley stood next to his friend. He looked down at his feet. "Does anyone else know?"

"No, not yet. It was a shock to see him. I could hardly believe it."

Father Cawley looked over at his fellow pastor. He tried to affect his normal non-assuming tone, "So...how did he look? When you saw him." He paused, "Seem to be getting along all right?"

Pastor Billings smiled slightly. The day was heating up but the sun felt good on his skin. It had been a huge relief going back to the mine alone to pay his respects to Davis. He had talked to the Lord about his own part in the burial, his concern about the unusual rush of events. and his knowledge that Tobias was watching him as the ceremony progressed. Something had been left undone.

So the pastor had returned. He had prayed by the shaft, straightened the little cross that Davis' family had propped up in the gravel and secured it with larger stones. He had read from Psalms.

Pastor Billings hadn't noticed Tobias until he turned to go. He thought at first he saw a spirit – the figure stood so tall, so erect. He had assumed the dog was dead. No one had seen him for awhile, no news of him from the sheriff who had kept the investigation open all summer, even making the 40 mile trip down to Ash Meadows to see if anyone at the refuge had seen the dog.

But no one had – not even the biologists who went out to record which animals were using the guzzlers – metal boxes set into the ground to hold rain water as well as water from the spring-fed reservoirs that bubbled up from the Amargosa. Not only protected species used the guzzlers; all wildlife was welcome to use them – coyotes and foxes, bighorn sheep, even the occasional bobcat or mountain lion, creatures that otherwise remained invisible, living undetected throughout the unfenced 23,000 acre refuge. If Tobias could survive any-where and not be found, it would be there.

However, the importance of finding Tobias was fading fast. Although Harold Pinehurst and a small posse of hunters still went out every now and then to search for him, by sum-mer's end they were more interested in other things. A sur-plus of wild turkeys was evident strolling in the high grasses along the Amargosa and hunting season would be open soon.

So with the cooling weather and September almost upon them, most of the locals, along with pastor Billings, had been losing interest in the phantom dog that had never been found. For some, the fate of Tobias, like the fate of Davis, was no longer of consequence. The dog was gone; it was over.

But here he was. Pastor Billings stared. He took a step, reached for his glasses, put them on, and looked more closely. It was Tobias, no doubt about it.

Someone must have cleaned him up, been caring for him. Pastor Billings had his suspicions about who that someone was.

He turned back to the Franciscan now, picking up the thread of conversation, "Looked all right, from what I could see. Still up there in that cave of his."

The Franciscan nodded. "Day and night. He lives there – won't leave it."

Pastor Paul lowered his voice. He took a step closer to Father Gene, looking down as he spoke, "The dog's an embarrassment, Gene. Watch some snoopy TV station go out there and get his picture, re-open the whole Davis event."

Father Gene looked past his fellow pastor toward the horizon. *Now that was an interesting idea.*

For a moment they were silent. When Pastor Billings spoke again his tone carried an intimacy, "What are you thinking, Gene? How are you making sense of it?"

"The Franciscan looked back at his friend. He sighed. "I'm not sure, Paul. I'm not sure why he's there."

"Know what I think?" Pastor Billings looked into the sun; the first of the Catholics were on their way down the road. "I think he's there to let us know that maybe we gave up too soon. There are people who claim Davis could have been saved – companies that go into old mines like that one all the time. But no one here reached out to them."

The pastor sighed. "Too proud, is how I see it. Couldn't admit that we needed their help. Might not have worked, but we should have tried. "

Pastor Paul looked down. Then after a moment he looked back at his friend. "I should have spoken up, Gene, especially when Pinehurst shot that dog. Two wrongs don't make a right. The dog looked right at me; he knew I should have spoken up.

Father Gene sighed quietly. "He wasn't sent here to judge us, Paul. He's just a dog."

"I know." Pastor Paul turned away. After a moment he turned back, the hint of a smile on his lips.

"Davis is safe with God now, and I won't worry about the dog as long as you don't. I only hope he gets another chance, Gene. Before it's too late."

Pastor Paul looked at his friend with a look that Father Gene would never forget. "Just one more chance," he said quietly. To disappear like he always does. To live his life. To walk away."

But the conversation was over. They both knew that, in earthly terms, Tobias had no chance at all.

CHAPTER 17

But we have to keep trying, don't we. We have to send our messages:

DOG KEEPS WATCH
AT
ABANDONED MINE

It was eight a.m. Harold was at his favorite spot, the small round table outside the service station at the edge of town. He placed his coffee down carefully and opened the county newspaper. And just like that – there it was: all of it, the little cross at the sealed entrance to the shaft where Davis fell, and the story beneath:

The Sad Tale Of A Man Left To Die and the
faithful dog that would not abandon him

But the real shocker was the photo of Tobias, standing tall on his hill above Davis' tomb with no sign of injury, his coat a reddish bronze, his demeanor proud and alert.

"No way … no way," Harold bent low over the photo. "He don't even look like that. Photo-shopped him, that's what they done, made him look young. I'll wager that's not even Tobias."

But it was Tobias, all right. And the story went viral.

It wasn't long before the entire country wanted to help, descending upon the little town en masse, sending a confused Harold back to his cabin to sulk.

Reporters from all of the major news outlets filled the two small motels. Television crews from New York and Los Angeles arrived eager to get a shot of the magnificent dog guarding the tomb of his unfortunate friend. Crews from Canada, South America and Europe set up their tents at the mine, all hoping for a glimpse of Tobias.

Talk of recovery filled the news. There were offers of equipment that could reach down 1200 feet, claws that could lift out rotted timber easily, grasping the pieces of ancient supports that had crumbled and blocked the shaft. The work would be swift and clean – no breaking out rock that could create slides of dust and debris, only the expertise of those with years of experience in the underground workings of ancient mines.

Soon it was happening. Earthmovers were on the way, rolling down the highway on flatbeds, traveling from Winnemucca, from Elko, heavy drums with hundreds of feet of steel cable, apparatus for lighting, meshed wire sheeting and, as an extra precaution, heavy boards to wedge under hanging walls to lessen the danger of rockfalls.

Finally a completely enclosed cylindrical cage that could be safely lowered to retrieve the body, to bring Davis up into the light and to give him the decent burial that every man deserves.

Throughout the confusion that followed, Mira and Ben stayed home at the campsite. Mira kept the photo of Tobias from the local paper under her pillow.

"He looks so beautiful," she told her father, the day that the paper first came out. "Dad, Remember the night that he came to us?"

"I remember," Jacob was busy at his work.

"Well, I understand now," she continued, speaking softly but with such intensity that Jacob stopped what he was doing and looked at his daughter with whole-hearted concern.

"You do? ..." His voice trailed off.

Mira nodded. "I understand why he couldn't stay with us anymore. He had to go back to the mine. He had to watch over Davis. That was his job all along. He had to save Davis … from being lonely."

Mira was standing next to her father. She leaned her head against him and for a moment neither moved.

"Toby knows about lonely," she said quietly.

The greatest mystery, however, for most of the town, the county, even the state, was not why Tobias was guarding the mine. The most intriguing enigma was how Toby had survived those many months unseen. Why hadn't he bled to death when Harold had shot him? Why hadn't he died from his injuries long ago?

Wasn't he starving, barely able to walk? Wouldn't he have come closer to town to look for help, or disappeared forever into the hills to stay as far away as possible from those who had hurt him? Why wasn't he afraid?

But it wasn't really a mystery. Mira knew this. Father Gene's smile and his gentle voice explained it all. "An angel was with him," he told her quietly, "right beside him the whole time."

"Did you see her?" Mira had whispered.

"No," Father Gene had answered. "Let's just say ... I felt her. I felt that she was there."

In the meantime Tobias was becoming a legend. There were photos, but not many. They showed clear eyes, strong shoulders, a silky golden coat with sliding patches of bronze and a long tail that wrapped around him where he lay on his hill above Davis' tomb.

There was no sign of injury in the photos, no sign that he had ever been shot. So that most locals agreed with Harold that the current photos had been altered. But there was no way to be sure of this because Tobias disappeared the same day that the earthmovers began arriving.

It was Davis' sister who found Mira and who sat down with Jacob and the family at their campsite and wept until no tears were left. They welcomed her, invited her to stay, embraced her when she needed comfort.

Later, as she sat with them around their small campfire, she asked Mira about her brother's backpack, if anything had been found that could have fallen out because it had been returned to her empty.

So Mira told her about the sandwich she and Ben had found, wrapped in brown paper, not far from the shaft, behind some rocks. She said that she had taken the sandwich up to Toby's cave and left it there for him, although she wasn't sure why she did this because everyone said that the dog was dead.

It was a still night, no wind, a sky full of stars. The fire cast a golden light on the group around the fire as Davis' sister quietly asked Mira if perhaps Toby would like to come home with her because he was the only one who had stayed true to her brother and who had befriended him in his hour of need.

And Mira looked across the fire and … she saw Tobias. He was right there with them, his copper coat full and lustrous, his long tail wrapped around him. And Mira's eyes filled with tears as she saw Davis' sister move and sit beside him.

Davis sister fell asleep by Tobias that night, and as the fire became a glow of orange embers, she laid her head on him, and he laid his head over hers. And Tobias felt her tears and her pain. And he remembered. And he understood.

CHAPTER 18

"Well, looks like he's finally gone for good." Harold Pinehurst reclined his tattered chaise a notch, put his unopened can of beer safely within arm's reach on the ground beside him and looked up at the sprawling desert sunset.

"Truth is I'm glad it worked out like it did." For a moment Harold reflected. "Maybe one of them crane operators took the dog, or someone from the mining company."

Father Gene followed his friend's example, leaning back in his lawn chair, propping his feet on the orange crate that served as a table for Harold's more important guests. He looked up at the sky. "Putting on a show for us tonight, Hal. Visitors don't know what we got up here."

Harold Pinehurst took a moment to scan the vast display of changing light above them, the deepening gold, the blazing scarlet of autumn's end and winters sure approach, "Got that right." He sighed, "Wouldn't want to live anywhere else."

After a moment he spoke again, "There's a rumor that the dog died; the family found his body out in the desert, took it with them back to California.

"Seems they left it at that little chapel right on the edge of Death Valley, made a little grave for him. Know anything about that?"

Harold paused, "That's one of the places on your circuit, that little town with the chapel. Am I right, Father?"

Father Cawley was quiet. His eyes were closed so Harold continued. It was dusk now, a smoky autumn dusk. "They say a coyote– a female, comes and lays beside his grave like how he laid with Davis. Makes my skin crawl, Father." Harold paused. "Course, it's just a story. I don't believe it."

A few minutes later, he sat up straighter and looked over at Father Gene. He felt quite sure the Franciscan was asleep, or almost asleep, so he relaxed. It felt safer to this way. He could take his time.

"I know what I did was wrong, Father. It's time I said it;" Harold waited a moment but the Franciscan's eyes remained closed.

"I never should have shot that dog." Harold was mumbling now, talking mostly to himself. After a moment of silence, he added softly, "You can tell the Lord I'm sorry, Father. And I'm hoping that Davis can rest in peace."

Father Gene nodded slowly. After a few moments he opened his eyes, just slightly. The desert dusk moved like a cloak of velvet against his skin. "And may that old dog rest in peace too," he prayed quietly.

"Amen to that, Father Gene," he heard Harold say in a voice just above a whisper. "Amen to that."

While miles away under a full moon that shone its pale light upon the desert floor, a coyote female with a soft buff color coat moved silently across the land.

She stopped on a low hill behind a small white chapel. A carefully inscribed stone lay before her. No dates were on the stone – only this:

TOBIAS
SAFE WITH GOD
REMEMBER US

The coyote sat quietly beside the stone. For a moment she looked out across the night as if expecting someone. And then she lay down peacefully and sighed. She would keep watch.

finis

HISTORICAL NOTE

This book is fiction. However, it is important to acknowledge that a similar tragedy to the mining disaster described here, actually occurred in northern Nevada in 2011.

In light of this actual tragedy, the family of Devin Westenskow is respectfully acknowledged both for the immense suffering they endured and for the courage they demonstrated when Devin's rescue from the shaft of the abandoned mine into which he fell was suspended.

This suspension was considered necessary because of the proven instability of the shaft which, if further disturbed by those trying to save Mr, Westenskow could easily collapse and kill them all.

In detailing the fictional event, no attempt is made by the author of A *Prayer for Tobias* to pass judgment on this decision. This was a tragedy that deeply affected everyone involved.

Following is a brief excerpt from *Tobias Returns*

A CALL FOR HELP

CHAPTER 1

This was Tobias. And so ... he wasn't dead; he couldn't be dead. The remains they had buried could have been any skinny long-haired dog who had his stomach crushed, his legs torn loose, his head blown apart by a tremendous unknown force. Her father said it was Tobias. Everyone said it was Tobias. But Mira didn't believe it. She pretended to believe it but in her deepest heart, she couldn't.

They had performed the proper ritual however. They had grieved over the poor dog they had found, keeping him with them until they were packed up and leaving the Nevada campsite that had been their home for almost a year.

They buried him in a box with Tobias' blanket, Tobias' favorite rawhide bone, the comb they had used to patiently pull out his burs, even the old rubber boot that he used as a toy. They said prayers over him, and they dug a resting place for him behind a little chapel on Death Valley's edge with only empty desert and miles of sky to form a cathedral of peace around him.

They did all that for the dog they had found. And it was good to do it. And they were glad they did it. But it wasn't Tobias.

TO BE CONTINUED ....

FROM THE AUTHOR

Did you enjoy this book? Why not leave a brief comment on social media or on the page from which you purchased it? This helps others feel good about giving it a try.

IMPORTANT NOTICE: THE SEQUEL TO THIS BOOK, *TOBIAS RETURNS,* WILL BE AVAILALE IN A PRINT EDITION BY WINGSPAN PRESS IN SEPTEMBER 2017.

Happy reading!
Bobbi Boland White
bbwmanagement@aol.com